Alan Green had to think of a plan to get to Estorya and to the demons' iron vessel—which was obviously a spaceship. It was his only chance. Soon the rainy season would start and there would be no vessels leaving for at least three months.

He could, of course, just walk away and hope to get to Estorya on foot. Thousands of miles through countless perils...

PHILIP JOSÉ FARMER
THE GREEN ODYSSEY

BERKLEY BOOKS, NEW YORK

This Berkley book contains the complete
text of the hardcover edition.
It has been completely reset in a typeface
designed for easy reading, and was printed
from new film.

THE GREEN ODYSSEY

A Berkley Book / published by arrangement with
Gregg Press, A Division of G. K. Hall & Co.

PRINTING HISTORY
Ballantine Books edition published 1957
Gregg Press edition / June 1978
Berkley edition / September 1983

ISBN: 0-425-06159-0

A BERKLEY BOOK ® TM 757,375
Berkley Books are published by The Berkley Publishing Group,
200 Madison Avenue, New York, New York 10016.
The name "BERKLEY" and the stylized "B" with design
are trademarks belonging to Berkley Publishing Corporation.
PRINTED IN THE UNITED STATES OF AMERICA

To Nan Gerding

Make friends fast.

—Handbook for the Shipwrecked

1

FOR TWO YEARS Alan Green had lived without hope. From the day the spaceship had crashed on this unknown planet he had resigned himself to the destiny created for him by accident and mathematics. Chances against another ship landing within the next hundred years were a million to one. Therefore it would do no good to sit around waiting for rescue. Much as he loathed the idea, he must live the rest of his life here, and he must squeeze as much blood as he could out of this planet-sized turnip. There wasn't much to squeeze. In fact, it seemed to him that he was the one losing the blood. Shortly after he'd been cast away he'd been made a slave.

Now, suddenly, he had hope.

Hope came to him a month after he'd been made foreman of the kitchen slaves of the Duke of Tropat. It came to him as he was standing behind the Duchess during a meal and directing those who were waiting upon her.

It was the Duchess Zuni who had not so subtly maneuvered him from the labor pens to his coveted, if dangerous, position. Why dangerous? Because she was very jealous and possessive, and the slightest hint of lack of attention from him could mean he'd lose his life or one limb or another. The knowledge of what had happened to his two predecessors kept him extremely sensitive to her every gesture, her every wish.

That fateful morning he was standing behind her as she sat at one end of the long breakfast table. In one hand he held his foreman's wand, a little white baton topped by a large red ball. With it he gestured at the slaves who served food, who poured wine and beer, who fanned away the flies, who carried in the household god and sat it on the god chair, who played something like music. Now and then he bent over the Duchess Zuni's long black hair and whispered phrases from this or that love poem, praising her beauty, her supposed unattainability, and his burning, if seemingly hopeless, passion for her. Zuni would smile, or repeat the formula of thanks—the short one—or else giggle at his funny accent.

The Duke sat at the other end of the table. He ignored the byplay, just as he ignored the so-called secret passage inside the walls of the castle, which Green used to get to the Duchess's apartments. Custom demanded this, just as custom demanded that he should play the outraged husband if she got tired of Green or angry at him and accused him publicly of amorous advances. This was enough to make Green jittery, but he had more than the Duke to consider. There was Alzo.

Alzo was the Duchess's watchdog, a mastifflike monster with shaggy red-gold hair. The dog hated Green with a vindictiveness that Green could only account for by supposing that the animal knew, perhaps from his body odor, that he was not a native of this planet. Alzo rumbled a warning deep in his chest every time Green bent over the Duchess or made a too-sudden movement. Occasionally he rose to his four feet and nuzzled the man's leg. When that happened Green could not keep from breaking out into a sweat, for the dog had twice bitten him, playfully, so to speak, and severely lacerated his calf. As if that weren't bad enough, Green had to worry that the natives might notice that his scars healed abnormally fast, almost overnight. He'd been forced to wear bandages on his legs long after the new skin had come in.

Even now, the nauseating canine was sniffing around Green's quivering hide in the hope of putting the fear of the devil in him. At that moment the Earthman resolved that, come the headsman's ax, rack, wheel, or other hellish tortures, he was going to kill that hound. It was just after he made that vow that the Duchess caused him to forget altogether the beast.

"Dear," said Zuni, interrupting the Duke in the midst of his conversation with a merchant-captain, "what is this I hear about two men who have fallen from the sky in a great ship of iron?"

Green quivered, and he held his breath as he waited for the Duke's reply.

The Duke, a short, dark many-chinned man with white hair and very thick bristly salt-and-pepper eyebrows, frowned.

"Men? Demons, rather! Can men fly in an iron ship through the air? These two claimed to have come from the stars, and you know what that means. Remember Oixrotl's prophecy: *A demon will come, claiming to be an angel.* No doubt about these two! Just to show you their subtlety, they claim to be neither demon nor angels, but men! Now, there's devilish clever thinking. Confusing to anybody but the most clearheaded. I'm glad the King of Estorya wasn't taken in."

Eagerly Zuni leaned forward, her large brown eyes bright, and her red-painted mouth open and wet. "Oh, has he burned them already? What a shame! I should think he'd at least torture them for a while."

Miran, the merchant-captain, said, "Your pardon, gracious lady, but the King of Estorya has done no such thing. The Estoryan law demands that all suspected demons should be kept in prison for two years. Everybody knows that a devil can't keep his human disguise more than two years. At the end of that time he reverts to his natural flesh and form, a hideous sight to behold, blasphemous, repulsive, soul-shaking."

Miran rolled his one good eye so that only the white showed and made the sign to ward off evil, the index finger held rigidly out from a clenched fist. Jugkaxtr, the household priest, dived under the table, where he crouched praying, secure in the knowledge that demons couldn't touch him while he knelt beneath the thrice-blessed wood. The Duke swallowed a whole glass of wine, apparently to calm his nerves, and belched.

Miran wiped his face and said, "Of course, I wasn't able to find out much, because we merchants are regarded with deep suspicion and scarcely dare to move outside the harbor or the marketplace. The Estoryans worship a female deity— ridiculous, isn't it?—and eat fish. They hate us Tropatians because we worship Zaxropatr, Male of Males, and because they must depend on us to bring them fish. But they aren't close-mouthed. They babble on and on to us, especially when one has given them wine for nothing."

Green finally released his breath in a sigh of relief. How glad he was that he had never told these people his true origin! So far as they knew he was merely one of the many slaves who came from a distant country in the North.

Miran cleared his throat, adjusted his violet turban and yellow robes, pulled gently at the large gold ring that hung from his nose and said, "It took me a month to get back from Estorya, and that is very good time indeed, but then I am noted for my good luck, though I prefer to call it skill plus the favor given by the gods to the truly devout. I do not boast, O gods, but merely give you tribute because you have smiled upon my ventures and have found pleasing the scent of my many sacrifices in your nostrils!"

Green lowered his eyelids to conceal the expression of disgust which he felt must be shining from them. At the same time, he saw Zuni's shoe tapping impatiently. Inwardly he groaned, because he knew she would divert the conversation to something more interesting to her, to her clothes and the state of her stomach and/or complexion. And there would be nothing that anybody could do about it, because the custom was that the woman of the house regulated the subject of talk during breakfast. If only this had been lunch or dinner! Then the men would theoretically have had uncontested control.

"These two demons were very tall, like your slave Green, here," said Miran, "and they could not speak a word of Estoryan. Or at least they claimed they couldn't. When King Raussmig's soldiers tried to capture them they brought from the folds of their strange clothes two pistols that only had to be pointed to send silent and awesome and sure death. Everywhere men dropped dead. Panic overtook many, but there were brave soldiers who kept on charging, and eventually the magical instruments became exhausted. The demons were overpowered and put into the Tower of Grass Cats from which no man or demon has yet escaped. And there they will be until the Festival of the Sun's Eye. Then they will be burnt..."

From beneath the table rose the babble of the priest, Jugkaxtr, as he blessed everyone in the house, down to the

latest-born pup, and the fleas living thereof, and cursed all
those who were possessed by even the tiniest demon. The
Duke, growing impatient at the noise, kicked under the
table. Jugkaxtr yelped and presently crawled out. He sat
down and began gnawing the meat from a bone, a well-
done-thou-good-and-faithful-servant expression on his fat
features. Green also felt like kicking him, just as he often
felt like kicking every single human being on this planet.
It was hard to remember that he must exercise compassion
and understanding for them, and that his own remote ancestors had once been just as nauseatingly superstitious,
cruel and bloody.

There was a big difference between reading about such
people and actually living among them. A history or a romantic novel could describe how unwashed and diseased
and formula-bound primitives were, but only the too-too
substantial stench and filth could make your gorge rise.

Even as he stood there Zuni's powerful perfume rose and
clung in heavy festoons about him and slithered down his
nostrils. It was a rare and expensive perfume, brought back
by Miran from his voyages and given to her as a token of
the merchant's esteem. Used in small quantities it would
have been quite effective to express feminine daintiness and
to hint at delicate passion. But no, Zuni poured it like water
over her, hoping to cover up the stale odor left by *not* taking
a bath more than once a month.

She looked so beautiful, he thought. And stank so terribly. At least she had at first. Now she looked less beautiful
because he knew how stupid she was, and didn't stink quite
so badly because his nostrils had become somewhat adjusted. They'd had to.

"I intend to be back in Estorya by the time of the festival,"
said Miran. "I've never seen the Eye of the Sun burn demons
before. It's a giant lens, you know. There will be just time
enough to make a voyage there and get back before the

rainy season. I expect to make even greater profits than the last time, because I've established some highly placed contacts. O gods, I do not boast but merely praise your favor to your humble worshiper, Miran the Merchant of the Clan of Effenycan!"

"Please bring me some more of this perfume," said the Duchess, "and I just love the diamond necklace you gave me."

"Diamonds, emeralds, rubies!" cried Miran, kissing his hand and rolling his eye ecstatically. "I tell you, the Estoryans are rich beyond our dreams! Jewels flow in their marketplaces like drops of water in a cataract! Ah, if only the Emperor could be induced to organize a great raiding fleet and storm its walls!"

"He remembers too well what happened to his father's fleet when he tried it," growled the Duke. "The storm that destroyed his thirty ships was undoubtedly raised by the priests of the Goddess Hooda. I still think that the expedition would have succeeded, however, if the late Emperor had not ignored the vision that came to him the night before they set sail. It was the great god Axoputqui, and he said . . ."

There was a lengthy conversation which did not hold Green's attention. He was too busy trying to think of a plan whereby he could get to Estorya and to the demons' iron vessel, which was obviously a spaceship. This was his only chance. Soon the rainy season would start and there would be no vessels leaving for at least three months.

He could, of course, just walk away and hope to get to Estorya on foot. Thousands of miles through countless perils, and he had only a general idea of where the city was . . . no, Miran was his only hope.

But how . . . ? He didn't think that stowing away would work. There was always a careful search for slaves who might try just that very plan. He looked at Miran, the short, fat, big-stomached, hook-nosed, one-eyed fellow with many chins and a large gold ring in his nose. The fellow was shrewd, shrewd, and he would not want to offend the Duchess by helping her official gigolo escape. Not, that is, unless Green could offer him something that was so valuable that he couldn't afford not to take the risk. Miran boasted that he was a hard-headed businessman, but it was Green's observation that there was always a large soft spot in that supposedly impenetrable cranium: the Fissure of Cupiditas.

2

THE DUKE ROSE, and everybody followed his example. Jugkaxtr chanted the formula of dismissal then sat down to finish gnawing on the bone. The others filed out. Green walked in front of Zuni in order to warn her of any obstacles in her path and to take the brunt of any attempted assassination. As he did so he was seized by the ankle and tripped headlong. He did not fall hard because he was a quick man, in spite of his six-foot-two and hundred ninety pounds. But he rose red-faced because of the loud laughter and from repressed anger at Alzo, who had again repeated his trick of grabbing Green's leg and upsetting him. He wanted to grab a spear from a nearby guard and spit Alzo. But that would be the end of Green. And whereas up to now there had been many times when he would not particularly have cared if he left this planet via the death route, he could not now make a false move. Not when escape was so near!

So he grinned sheepishly and again preceded the Duchess, while the others followed her out. When they reached the bottom of the broad stone staircase that led to the upper floors of the castle, Zuni told Green that he was to go to the marketplace and buy tomorrow's food. As for her, she was going back to bed and sleep until noon.

Inwardly Green groaned. How long could he keep up this pace? He was expected to stay up half the night with her, then attend to his official duties during the day. She slept enough to be refreshed by the time he visited her, but he never had a chance for any real rest. Even when he had his free hours in the afternoon he had to go to his house in the pens, and there he had to stay awake and attend to all his familial duties. And Amra, his slave-wife, and her six children demanded much from him. They were even more tyrannical than the Duchess, if that were possible.

How long, O Lord, how long? The situation was intolerable; even if he'd not heard of the spaceship he would have plotted to escape. Better a quick death while trying to get away than a slow, torturous one by exhaustion.

He bowed good-by to the Duke and Duchess, then followed the violet turban and yellow robes of Miran through the courtyard, through the thick stone walls, over the bridge of the broad moat, and into the narrow winding streets of the city of Quotz. Here the merchant-captain got into his silver-and-jewel-decorated rickshaw. The two long-legged men between its shafts, sailors and clansmen from Miran's vessel, the *Bird of Fortune,* began running through the crowd. The people made way for them, as two other sailors preceded them calling out Miran's name and cracking whips in the air.

Green, after looking to make certain that nobody from the castle was around to see him, ran until he was even with the rickshaw. Miran halted it and asked what he wanted.

"Your pardon, Your Richness, but may a humble slave speak and not be reprimanded?"

"I presume it is no idle thought you have in mind," said Miran, looking Green over his one eye narrow in its fat-folds.

"It has to do with money."

"Ah, despite your foreign accent you speak with a pleasing voice; you are the golden trumpet of Mennirox, my patron god. Speak!"

"First Your Richness must swear by Mennirox that you will under no circumstances divulge my proposal."

"There is wealth in this? For me?"

"There is."

Miran glanced at his clansmen, standing there patiently, apparently oblivious of what was going on. He had power of life and death over them, but he didn't trust them. He said, "Perhaps it would be better if I thought about this before making such a drastic oath. Could you meet me tonight at the Hour of the Wineglass at the House of Equality? And could you perhaps give me a slight hint of what you have in mind?"

"The answer to both is yes. My proposal has to do with the dried fish that you carry as cargo to the Estoryans. There is another thing, too, but I may not even hint at it until I have your oath."

"Very well then. At the agreed hour. Fish, eh? I must be off. Time is money, you know. Get going boys, full sails."

Green hailed a passing rickshaw and seated himself comfortably in it. As assistant majordomo he had plenty of money. Moreover, the Duke and Duchess would have been outraged if he had lowered their prestige by walking through the city's streets. His vehicle made good time, too, because everybody recognized his livery: the scarlet and white tricorn hat and the white sleeveless shirt with the Duke's heraldic arms on its chest—red and green concentric circles pierced by a black arrow.

The street led always downward, for the city had been built on the foothills of the mountains. It wandered here and there and gave Green plenty of time to think.

The trouble was, he thought, that if the two imprisoned men at Estorya were to die before he got to them he'd still be lost. He had no idea of how to pilot or navigate a spaceship. He'd been a passenger on a freighter when it had unaccountably blown up, and he'd been forced to leave the dying vessel in one of those automatic castaway emergency shells. The capsule had got him down to the surface of this planet and was, as far as he knew, still up in the hills where he'd left it. After wandering for a week and almost starving to death he'd been picked up by some peasants. They had turned him in to the soldiers of a nearby garrison, thinking he must be a runaway slave on whom they'd collect a reward. Taken to the capital city of Quotz, Green had almost been freed because there was no record of his being anybody's property. But his tallness, blondness and inability to speak the local language had convinced his captors that he must have wandered down from some far northern country. Therefore if he wasn't a slave he should be.

Presto, changeo! He was. And he'd put in six months in a quarry and a year as a dock worker. Then the Duchess had chanced to see him on the streets as she rode by, and he'd been transferred to the castle.

The streets were alive with the short, dark, stocky natives and the taller, lighter-complexioned slaves. The former wore their turbans of various colors, indicating their status and trade. The latter wore their three-cornered hats. Occasionally a priest in his high conical hat, hexagonal spectacles and goatee rode by. Wagons and rickshaws drawn by men or by big, powerful dogs went by. Merchants stood at the fronts of their shops and hawked their wares in loud voices. They sold cloth, *grixtr* nut, parchment, knives, swords, helmets, drugs, books—on magic, on religion, on travel— spices, perfumes, ink, rugs, highly sugared drinks, wine, beer, tonic, paintings, everything that went to make up their civilization. Butchers stood before open shops where dressed fowl, deer and dogs hung. Dealers in birds pointed out the virtues of their many-colored and multi-songed pets.

For the thousandth time Green wondered at this strange planet where the only large animals were men, dogs, grass cats, a small deer and a very small equine. In fact, there was a paucity of any variety of animal life, except for the surprisingly large number of birds. It was this scarcity of horses and oxen, he supposed, that helped perpetuate slavery. Man and dog had to provide most of the labor.

No doubt there was an explanation for all this, but it must be buried so deep in this people's forgotten history that one would never know. Green, always curious, wished that he had time and means to explore. But he didn't. He might as well resign himself to keeping a whole skin and to getting out of this mess as fast as he could.

There was enough to do merely to make his way through the narrow and crowded streets. He had to display his baton often to clear a path, though when he approached the harbor area he had less trouble because the streets were much wider.

Here great wagons drawn by gangs of slaves carried huge loads to or from the ships. The thoroughfares had to be broad, else the people would have been crushed between wagon and house. Here also were the so-called Pens, where the dock-slaves lived. Once the area had actually been an enclosure where men and women were locked up for the night. But the walls had been torn down and new houses built in the old Duke's time. The closest Earthly parallel

Green could think of for these edifices was a housing project. Small cottages, all exactly alike, set in military columns.

For a moment he considered stopping off to see Amra, then decided against it. She'd get him tied up in an argument or something, and he'd spend too much time trying to soothe her, time that should be spent at the marketplace. He hated scenes, whereas Amra was a born self-dramatist who reveled in them, almost wallowed, one might say.

He averted his eyes from the Pens and looked at the other side of the street, where the walls of the great warehouses towered. Workmen swarmed around them, and cranes, operated by gangs pushing wheels like a ship's capstan, raised or lowered big bundles. Here, he thought, was a business opportunity for him.

Introduce the steam engine. It'd be the greatest thing that ever hit this planet. Wood-burning automobiles could replace the rickshaws. Cranes could be run by donkey-engines. The ships themselves could have their wheels powered by steam. Or perhaps, he thought, rails could be laid across the Xurdimur, and locomotives would make the ships obsolete.

No, that wouldn't work. Iron rails cost too much. And the savages that roved over the grassy plains would tear them up and forge weapons from them.

Besides, every time he suggested to the Duke a new and much more efficient method of doing something he ran dead into the brick wall of tradition and custom. Nothing new could be accepted unless the gods accepted it. The gods' will was interpreted by the priests. The priests clutched the status quo as tightly as a hungry infant clutches its mother's breast or an old man clings to his property.

Green could make a fight against the theocracy, but he didn't feel it was worthwhile to become a martyr.

He heard a familiar voice behind him calling his name.

"Alan! Alan!"

He hunched his shoulders like a turtle withdrawing his head and thought desperately for a moment of trying to ignore the voice. But, though a woman's, it was powerful and penetrating, and everybody around him had already turned to see its owner. So he couldn't pretend he hadn't heard it.

"ALAN, YOU BIG BLOND NO-GOOD HUNK OF MAN, STOP!"

Reluctantly Green told his rickshaw boy to turn around. The boy, grinning, did so. Like everybody else along the harbor front he knew Amra and was familiar with her relations with Green. She held their one-year-old daughter in her arms, cradled against her magnificent bosom. Behind her stood her other five children, her two sons by the Duke, her daughter by a visiting prince, her son by the captain of a Northerner ship, her daughter by a temple sculptor. Her rise and fall and slow rise again was told in the children around her; the tableau embodied an outline of the structure of the planet's society.

3

HER MOTHER had been a Northerner slave; her father, a native freeman, a wheelwright. When she was five years old they had died in a plague. She had been transferred to the Pens and raised by her aunt. When she was fifteen her beauty had attracted the Duke and he had installed her in the palace. There she gave birth to his two sons, now ten and eleven, who would soon be taken away from her and raised in the Duke's household as free and petted servants.

The Duke had married the present Duchess several years after his liaison with Amra began and her jealousy had forced him to get rid of Amra. Back to the Pens she had gone; perhaps the Duke had not been too sad to see her go, for living with her was like living with a hurricane, and he liked peace and quiet too well.

Then, in accordance with the custom, she had been recommended by the Duke to a visiting prince; the prince had overstayed his leave from his native country because he hated to part with her, and the Duke had wanted to give her as a present. But here he'd overstepped his legal authority. Slaves had certain rights. A woman who had borne a citizen a child could not be shipped away or sold unless she gave her permission. Amra didn't choose to go, so the sorrowing prince had gone home, though not without leaving a memento of his visit behind him.

The captain of a ship had purchased her, but here again the law came to her rescue. He could not take her out of the country, and she again refused to leave. By now she had purchased several businesses—slaves were allowed to hold property and even have slaves of their own—and she knew that her two boys by the Duke would be valuable later on, when they'd go to live with him.

The temple sculptor had used her as his model for his great marble statue of the goddess of Fertility. Well he might, for she was a magnificent creature, a tall woman with long, richly auburn hair, a flawless skin, large russet brown eyes, a mouth as red and ripe as a plum, breasts with which neither child nor lover could find fault, a waist amazingly slender considering the rest of her curved body and her fruitfulness. Her long legs would have looked good on an Earthwoman and were even more outstanding among a population of club-ankled females.

There was more to her than beauty. She radiated a something that struck every male at first sight; to Green she sometimes seemed to be a violent physical event, perhaps even a principle of Nature herself.

There were times when Green felt proud because she had picked him as her mate, chosen him when he was a newly imported slave who could say only a few words in the highly irregular agglutinative tongue. But there were times when he felt that she was too much for him, and those times had been getting too frequent lately. Besides, he felt a pang whenever he saw their child, because he loved it and dreaded the moment when he would have to leave it. As for deserting Amra, he wasn't sure how that would make him feel. Undeniably, she did affect him, but then so did a blow in the teeth or wine in the blood.

He got down out of the rickshaw, told the boy to wait, said, "Hello, honey," and kissed her. He was glad she was a slave, because she didn't wear a nose-ring. When he kissed the Duchess he was always annoyed by hers. She refused to take it off when with him because that would put her on his level, and he mustn't ever forget he was a slave. It was perfectly moral for her to take a bondsman as a lover but not a freeman, and she was nothing if not moral.

Amra's return kiss was passionate, part of which was the vigor of asperity. "You're not fooling me," she said. "You meant to ride right by. Kiss the children! What's the matter, are you getting tired of me? You told me you only accepted the Duchess's offer because it meant advancement, and you were afraid that if you turned her down she'd find an excuse to kill you. Well, I believed you—half-believed you, anyway. But I won't if you try sneaking by without seeing me. What's the matter? Are you a man or not? Are you afraid to face a woman? Don't shake your head. You're a liar! Don't forget to kiss Grizquetr; you know he's an affectionate boy and worships you, and it's absurd to say that in your country grown men don't kiss boys that old. You're not in your country—what a strange, frigid, loveless race must live there—and even if you were you might overlook their customs to show some tenderness to the boy. Come on back to our house and I'll bring up some of that wonderful Chalousma wine that came in the other day out of the cellar——"

"What was a ship doing in your cellar?" he said, and he whooped with laughter. "By all the gods, Amra, I know it's been two days since I've seen you, but don't try to crowd forty-eight hours' conversation into ten minutes, especially your kind of conversation. And quit scolding me in front of the children. You know it's bad for them. They might pick up your attitude of contempt for the head of the house."

"I? Contempt? Why, I worship the ground you walk on! I tell them continually what a fine man you are, though it's rather hard to convince them when you do show up and they see the truth. Still . . ."

There was only one way to handle her; that was to outtalk, outshout, outact her. It was hard going, especially when he felt so tired, and when she would not cooperate with him but would fight for precedence. The trouble was, she didn't feel any respect for the man she could shut up, so it was absolutely necessary to dominate her.

This he accomplished by giving her a big squeeze, causing the baby to cry because she was pushed in too tightly between the two of them. Then while Amra was trying to soothe the baby he began telling her what had happened at the palace.

She was silent, except for a sharply pointed question interjected now and then, and she insisted upon hearing the details of everything that had taken place—everything. He told her things that he would not have mentioned before children—two years ago. But the extremely frank and uninhibited society of the slaves had freed him of any such restraints.

They went inside Amra's house, through her offices, where six of her clerks and secretaries worked, through the living rooms proper, and on into the kitchen.

She rang a bell and told Inzax, a pretty little blonde, to go into the cellar and bring up a quart of Chalousma. One of the clerks popped his head in the kitchen door and told her that a Mr. Sheshyarvrenti, purser of an Andoonanarga vessel, wanted to see her about the disposition of some rare birds that she had ordered seven months before. He would deal with no one but her.

"Let him cool his heels for a while," she said. The clerk gulped and his head disappeared.

Green took Paxi, his daughter, and played with her while Amra poured their wine.

"This can go on only so long," she said. "I love you, and I'm not getting the attention I'm accustomed to. You should find some pretense to break off with the Duchess. I'm a vigorous woman who needs a lot of love. I want you here."

Green had nothing to lose by agreeing with her, since he planned to be leaving in a very short time. "You're right," he said. "I'll tell her as soon as I think up a good excuse." He fingered his neck at the place where a headsman's ax would come down. "It had better be a good one, though."

Amra seemed to glow all over with happiness. She held her glass up and said, "Here's to the Duchess. May demons carry her off."

"You'd better be careful, saying that before the children. You know that if they innocently repeated that to someone and it got back to the Duchess you'd be burned in the next witchhunt."

"Not my children!" she scoffed. "They're too clever. They take after their mother. They know when to keep their mouths shut."

Green gulped his wine and stood up. "I must go."

"You'll come home tonight? Surely the Duchess will let you out one night a week?"

"Not one single night. And I can't come here this evening because I'm to meet Miran the Merchant at the House of Equality. Business, you know."

"Oh, I know! You'll dillydally about the whole matter, and put off acting for one reason or another, and the first thing you know, years will go by, and——"

"If this keep up I'll be dead in six months," he said. "I'm *tired!* I have to get some sleep."

She changed instantly from anger to sympathy. "Poor dear, why don't you forget that appointment and sleep here until time to go back to the castle? I'll send a messenger to Miran telling him you're sick."

"No, this is something I just can't pass by."

"What is it?"

"It's of such a nature that telling you, or anybody, would spoil it."

"And just what could that be?" she demanded, angry again. "It concerns some woman, I'll bet!"

"My problem is keeping away from you women, not getting into more trouble. No, it's just that Miran has sworn me by all his gods to keep silent and of course I couldn't think of breaking a vow."

"I know your opinion of our gods," she said. "Well, go along with you! But I warn you, I'm an impatient woman; I'll give you a week to work on the Duchess, then I'm launching an attack myself."

"That won't be necessary," he said. He kissed her and the children and left. He congratulated himself on having delayed Amra that long. If he couldn't carry out his scheme in a week he was lost, anyway. He'd have to walk away from the city and out onto the Xurdimur, even if packs of wild dogs and man-eating grass cats and cannibalistic men and God knew what else did roam the grassy plains.

4

EVERY CITY AND VILLAGE of the Empire had its House of Equality, within whose walls distinctions of every type were abandoned. Green did not know the origin of the institution, but he recognized its value as a safety valve to blow off the extreme social pressure put on every class. Here the slave who did not dare open his mouth in the outside mundane world could curse his master to his face and go unpunished by the authorities. Of course, there was nothing to keep the master from retaliating in kind, for the slave also cast off his legal rights when he entered. Violence was not unknown here, though it was infrequent. Blood shed within these walls did not, theoretically, call for punishment. But any murderer would find that, though the police paid no attention to him, he'd have to deal with the slain one's relatives. Many feuds had had their origin and end here.

Green had excused himself after the evening meal, saying that he had to talk to Miran about getting some spices from Estorya. Also the merchant had mentioned that on his last trip he'd heard that a band of Estoryan hunters were going after the rare and beautiful *getzlen* bird and that he might find some for sale when he returned there. Zuni's face lit up, because she desired a *getzlen* bird even more than a chance to annoy her husband. Graciously she gave Green permission to leave.

Inwardly exultant, though outwardly pulling a long face that was supposed to suggest his sadness at having to leave the Duchess, he backed out of the dining room. Not very gracefully, for Alzo chose that moment to refuse to get out of Green's path. Green tumbled backward, sprawling over the huge mastiff, who snarled with anger and trembled with hypocritical indignation and bared his fangs with the intention of tearing Green apart. The Earthman did not try to rise, because he did not want to give Alzo an excuse for jumping him. Instead he bared his own teeth and snarled back. The hall roared with laughter and the Duke, holding his sides, tears running from his bulging eyes, rose and staggered over to where the two faced each other on all fours. He clutched Alzo's spike-studded collar and dragged him away, meanwhile choking out a command to Green to take off while the taking off was good.

Green swallowed his anger, thanked the Duke and left. Swearing that he'd rip the hound apart some day with his bare hands, the Earthman left for the House of Equality. It took all the long rickshaw ride to the temple for him to calm down.

The great central room with its three-story ceiling was full that night. Men in their long evening kilts and women in masks crowded around the gambling tables, the bars and the grudgestages. There was a large crowd around the platform on which two dealers in wheat were slugging it out to work off resentment arising from business disputes. But by far the greatest number had gathered to watch a husband-and-wife match. His left hand had been tied to his side, and she had been armed with a club. Thus equalized, they'd been given the word to go to it. So far the man had had the worst of the match, as bloody patches on his head and bruises on his arm showed. If he could get the club away from her he had the right to do what he wanted to her. But if she could break his free arm she had him at her complete mercy.

Green avoided the stage, because such barbarous doings made him sick. Looking for Miran, he finally found him rolling a pair of six-sided dice with another captain. This fellow wore the red turban and black robes of the Clan Axucan. He had just lost to Miran and was paying him sixty *iquogr*, a goodly sum even for a merchant-prince.

Miran took Green's arm, something he'd never have done outside the House, and led him off to a curtained booth where they could get as much privacy as they wished. He matched Green for drinks; Green lost, and Miran ordered a large pitcher of Chalousma.

"Nothing but the best for yours truly—whenever someone else is paying," Miran said jovially. "Now, I'm a great one for fun, but I'm here primarily for business. So—let's have your proposal at once, if you please."

"First I must have your solemn oath that you will tell absolutely no one what you hear in this booth. Second, that if you reject my idea you do not then use it later on. Third, that if you do accept you will never attempt later on to kill me or get rid of me and thus reap the profits."

Miran's face had been blank, but at the word "profits" it twisted into many folds and creases, all expressive of joy.

He reached into the huge purse he carried slung over his shoulder and pulled out a little golden idol of the patron deity of the Clan Effenycan. Putting his right hand upon its ugly head, he lifted his left and said, "I swear by Zacef-fucanquanr that I will obey your wishes in this matter. May he strike me with lice, leprosy, lecher's disease and lightning if I should break this, my solemn vow."

Satisfied, Green said, "First I want you to arrange for me to be aboard your windroller when you leave for Estorya."

Miran choked on his wine and coughed and sputtered until Green pounded his back.

"I do not ask that you give me passage *back*. Now, here's my idea. You plan to be taking a large cargo of dried fish because the Estoryans' religion requires that they eat them at every meal and because they use them in great quantities at their numerous festivals."

"True, true. Do you know, I've never been able to figure out why they should worship a fish-goddess. They live over five thousand miles from the sea, and there's no evidence that any of them have ever been to the sea. Yet, they demand saltwater fish, won't use the fish from a nearby lake."

"There're many mysteries about the Xurdimur. However, they needn't concern us. Now, do you know that the Estoryans' Book of Gods places much more ritual-power in freshly killed and cooked fish than in smoked fish? However, they've always had to be content with the dried fish the windrollers brought them. What price would they not pay for living seafish?"

Miran rubbed his palms together. "Indeed it does make one wonder . . . ?"

Green then outlined his idea. Miran sat stunned. Not at the audacity or originality of the plan, but because it was so obvious that he wondered why neither he nor anyone else had ever thought of it. He said so.

Green drank his wine and said, "I suppose that people wondered the same thing when the first wheel or bow and arrow were invented. So obvious, yet no one thought of them until then."

"Let me get this straight," said Miran. "You want me to buy a caravan of wagons, build water-tight tanks into them and use them to transport ocean fish back to here? Then the wagon bodies, with their contents, will be lifted onto my windroller and fitted into specially prepared racks—or perhaps, holes—on the mid-deck? Also, you will show me how to analyze sea water so that its formula may be sold to the Estoryans, and they can thus keep the fish alive in their own tanks?"

"That's right."

"Hmmm." Miran ran his fat, ring-studded finger over his hook nose and the square gold ornament hanging therefrom. His single eye glared pale-bluely at Green. The other was covered with a white patch to hide the emptiness left after a ball from a Ving musket had struck it.

"It's four weeks until the very last day on which I can set sail from here and still get to Estorya and back before the rains come. It's just barely possible to have the tanks built, get them convoyed down to the seashore, get the fish in and bring them back. Meantime, I can be having the deck altered. If my men work day and night we can make it."

"Of course, this is a one-shot proposition. You can't possibly keep a monopoly on the idea, once the first trip is over. Too many people are bound to talk, and the other captains will hear of it."

"I know; don't teach an Effenycan to suck eggs. But what if the fish should die?"

Green shrugged and spread out his palms. "A possibility. You're taking a tremendous gamble. But every voyage on the Xurdimur is, isn't it? How many windrollers come back? Or how many can boast your list of forty successful trips?"

"Not many," said Miran.

He slumped in his seat, brooding over his goblet of wine. His eye, sunk in ranges of fat, seemed to stare through Green. The Earthman pretended indifference, though his heart was pounding, and he controlled his breathing with difficulty.

"You're asking a great deal," Miran finally said. "If the Duke were to find out that I'd agreed to help a valued slave escape, I'd be tortured in a *most* refined way, and the Clan Effenycan would be stripped of all its rights to sail wind-rollers and would probably be exiled to its native hills. Or else would have to take to piracy. And that, despite all the glamorous stories you hear, is not a very well-paying profession."

"You'd make a killing in Estorya."

"True, but when I think of what the Duchess will do when she discovers you've fled the country! Ow, ow, ow!"

"There's no reason why you should be connected with my disappearance. A dozen craft leave the harbor every day. Besides, for all she'll know, I've gone the opposite way, over the hills and to the ocean. Or to the hills themselves, where many runaway slaves are."

"Yes, but I have to return to Tropat. And my clansmen, though notoriously tight-lipped when sober, are also, I must confess, notorious drunkards. Someone'd be sure to babble in the taverns."

"I'll dye my hair black, cut it short, like a Tzatlam tribesman, and sign on."

"You forget that you have to belong to my clan in order to be a crew member."

"Hmmm. Well, what about this adoption-by-blood routine?"

"What about it? I can't propose that unless you've done something spectacular and for the profit of the clan. Wait! Can you play any musical instrument?"

Promptly, Green lied. "Oh, I am a wonderful harpist. When I play I can soothe a hungry grass cat into lying down at my feet and licking my toes with pure affection."

"Excellent! Though it would not be an affection so pure, since it is well known that the grass cat considers a man's toes a great delicacy and always eats them first, even before the eyes. Listen well. Here is what you must do in four weeks' time, for if all goes well, or all goes ill, we set sail on the Week of the Oak, the Day of the Sky, the Hour of the Lark, a most propitious time. . . ."

5

To Green, the next three weeks seemed to have shifted to low gear, they crept by so slowly. Yet they should have raced by quickly enough, so full of schemes and plots were they. He had to advise Miran on the many technical details involved in building tanks for the fish. He had to keep the Duchess happy, an increasingly difficult job because it was impossible to pretend a one-hundred-per-cent absorption in her while his mind desperately looked for flaws in his plans, found oh, so many, and then as anxiously sought ways of repairing them. Nevertheless he knew it was vital that he not displease or bore her. Prison would forever ruin his chances.

Worst of all, Amra was getting suspicious.

"You're trying to conceal something from me," she told Green. "You ought to know better. I can tell when a man is deceiving me. There's something about the voice, the eyes, the way he makes love, though you've been doing very little of that. What are you plotting?"

"I assure you it's simply that I'm very tired," he said sharply. "All I want is some peace and quiet, a little rest and a little privacy now and then."

"Don't try to tell me that's all!"

She cocked her head to one side and squinted at him, managing somehow even in this grotesque attitude to look ravishingly beautiful.

Suddenly she said, "You wouldn't be thinking of running away, would you?"

For a second he became pale. Damn the woman anyway!

"Don't be ridiculous," he said, trying hard to keep his voice from cracking. "I'm much too aware of the penalties if I were caught. Besides, why should I want to run away? You are the most desirable woman I've ever known. (This was the truth.) Though you're not the easiest one in the world to live with. (A master understatement.) I would have gotten no place without you. (True; but he couldn't spend the rest of his life on this barbarous world.) And it is unthinkable that I would want to leave you." (Inexpressible, yes, but not unthinkable. He couldn't take her with him, for the simple reason that even if she would go she would never fit in his life on Earth. She'd be absolutely unhappy. Moreover, she'd not go anyway, because she'd refuse to abandon her children and would try to take them along, thus wrecking all his escape plans. He might just as well hire a brass band and march behind it out of the city and onto the windroller in the light of high noon.)

Nevertheless his conscience troubled him. If it was painful to leave Amra it was hell to leave Paxi, his daughter. For days he had considered taking her along with him, but eventually abandoned the idea. Trying to steal her from under Amra's fiercely watchful gaze was almost impossible.

Moreover, Paxi would miss her mother terribly, and he had no business exposing the baby to the risks of the voyage, which were many. Amra would be doubly hurt. Losing him would be bad enough, but to lose Paxi also...! No, he couldn't do that to her.

The outcome of this conversation with her was that she apparently dropped her suspicions. At least she never spoke of them again. He was glad of that, for it was impossible to keep entirely hidden his connection with the mysterious actions of Miran the Merchant. The whole city knew something was up. There was undoubtedly a lot of money tied up with this deal of the wagon caravan going to the seashore. But what did it all mean? Neither Miran nor Green would say a word, and while the Duke and Duchess might have used their authority to get the information from their slave, the Duke made no move. Miran had promised to let him in on a share of the profits, provided he gave the merchant a free hand and asked no questions. The Duke was quite content. He planned on spending the money to increase his collection of glass birds. He had ten large rooms of the castle glittering with his fantastic aviary: shining, silent and grotesquely beautiful, all products of the glassblowers of the fabulous city of Metzva Moosh, far, far away across the grassy sea of the Xurdimur.

Green was present when the Duke talked to Miran about it.

"Now, Captain, you must understand just exactly what I do want," warned the ruler, lifting a finger to emphasize the seriousness of his words. His eyes, usually deep-sunk in their fat, had widened to reveal large, brown and soulful orbs. The passion for his hobby shone forth. Nothing: good Chalousma wine, his wife, the torture of a heretic or run-away slave, could make him quiver and glitter with delight as much as the thought of the exquisitely wrought image of a Metzva Moosh bird.

"I want two or three, but no more because I can't afford more. All made by Izan Yushwa, the greatest of the glass-blowers. I'd particularly like any modeled after the bird-of-terror. . . ."

"But when I was last in Estorya I heard that Izan Yushwa was dying," said Miran.

"Excellent, excellent!" cried the Duke. "That will make everything recently created by him even more valuable! If he is dead now it is probable that the Estoryans, who control the export of the Mooshans will be putting a high price on anything of his that comes their way. That means that bid-ding will be high during the festival and that you must outbid any prospective buyers. By all means do so. Pay any price, for I must have something created by him in his last days!"

The Duke, Green realized, was so eager because of the belief that a part of a dying artist's soul entered into his latest creations when he died. These were called "soul-works" and brought ten times as much as anything else, even if the conception and execution were inferior to pre-vious works.

Sourly Miran said, "But you have given me no money to buy your birds."

"Of course not. You will lend me the sum, buy them yourself, and when you come back with them I will raise the money to repay you."

Miran didn't seem too happy, but Green knew that the fat merchant was already planning to charge the Duke double the purchase price. As for Green, he liked to see a man interested in a hobby, but he was disgusted because taxes would now be raised in order to allow the Duke to add to his collection.

The Duchess, bored as usual by her husband's conver-sation, suddenly said, "Honey, let's go hunting next week-end. I've been so restless lately, so unable to sleep nights. I think I've been cooped up too long in this dismal old place. My digestion has been so sluggish lately. I think I need the exercise and the fresh air." And she went into vivid detail about certain aspects of her gastrointestinal troubles. The Earthman, who'd thought he was hardened to this people's custom of dwelling on such matters, turned green.

At the suggestion of a hunt the Duke didn't exactly groan, but his eyes rolled upward in supplication to the gods. Until he had reached the age of thirty he had enjoyed a good hunt. But like most upper-class men of his culture, he rapidly put on flesh after thirty and became as sedentary as possible. The belief was that fat increased a man's life span. Also, a big belly and double chin were signs of aristocratic blood and a full purse. Unfortunately, along with this came an inevitable decline in vigor, which, coupled with the December-May marriages that their society expected of them, had given birth to another institution: the slave male companion of the rich man's young wife.

It was toward Green that the Duke looked. "Why not let him conduct the hunt?" he suggested hopefully. "I've so much business to take care of."

"Like sitting on your fat cushion and contemplating your glass birds," she said. "No!"

"Very well," he said, resignedly. "I've a slave in the workpens who's to be executed for striking a foreman. We'll use him as the quarry. But I think we ought to give him two weeks to build up his wind and legs. Otherwise it would hardly be sporting, you know."

The Duchess frowned. "No. I'm getting bored; I can't stand this inaction any longer."

She shot a glance at Green. He felt his stomach muscles contracting. Evidently she'd noticed his lukewarm interest in her. This hunt was partly to suggest to him that he'd be meeting a like fate unless he perked up and began to be more entertaining.

It wasn't that thought that made his heart sink. It was

that next weekend was when Miran's windroller raised sail and when he planned to be aboard it. Now, he'd be gone conducting the hunting party up in the hills.

Green looked appealingly at Miran, but the merchant's shoulders rose beneath the yellow robe as if to say, "What can I do?"

He was right. Miran couldn't suggest that he too go along on the hunt, and thus give Green a chance to slip aboard afterward. The day on which the *Bird of Fortune* was scheduled to leave the windbreak was absolutely the last date on which it could set sail. He couldn't afford to take the chance of being caught in the rains in the middle of the vast plains.

6

ALL THE NEXT DAY Green was too busy setting up the schedule of the hunting party to have time to be gloomy. But when night came he seemed to fold up inside himself. Could he pretend to be sick, too, and be left behind when the party set out?

No, for they would at once assume that he had been possessed by a demon and would pack him off to the Temple of Apoquoz, God of Healing. There he'd be under lock and key until he proved himself healthy. The terrible part about going to the Temple of Apoquoz was that it made death almost inevitable. If you didn't die of your own disease you caught somebody else's.

Green wasn't worried about catching any of the many diseases he'd be exposed to in the Temple. Like all men of terrestrial descent, he carried in his body a surgically implanted protoplasmic entity which automatically analyzed any invading microscopic organisms and/or viruses and manufactured antibodies to combat them. It lived in the space created by the removal of his appendix; when working to fulfill its mission it demanded food and radiated a heat that assured its host of its heartening presence. An increased appetite plus a slight fever indicated that it was killing off the disease and that within several hours it would success-fully repel any boarders. In the two years Green had been on the planet it had had to attack at least forty times; Green calculated that he would have been dead each and every time if it had not been for his symbiote.

Knowing this didn't help him. If he played sick he'd be locked up and couldn't get on the 'roller. If he went on the hunting party he missed the boat, too.

Suppose he were to disappear the night before the party, to hide on the windroller while the castle vainly looked for him?

Not very likely. The first thing that would occur to Zuni would be to order the windbreak closed and all 'rollers searched for a possible stowaway. And if that happened Miran would be so delayed that it was unlikely he'd sail. Even if he, Green, hid in Miran's cabin, where he would probably be safe, there would still be the inevitable and totally frustrating delay.

Then why not disappear several days earlier, so that Miran could have time to reload his cargo? He'd see the merchant tomorrow. If Miran fell in with his plans, Green would disappear four nights from this very night, which would leave three days for the windroller to be emptied and reloaded. Fortunately the tanks wouldn't have to be taken off, because any fool could see that the runaway wasn't hiding at the bottom among the fish.

Much relieved that he at least had a way open, if a very perilous one, Green relaxed. He was sitting on a bench along a walk on top of one of the castle walls. The sky was blazingly beautiful with stars larger than any seen from Earth. The great moon and the small moon had risen. The larger had just cleared the eastern horizon and the lesser one was just past the zenith. Mingled moonwash and star-wash softened the grimness and ugliness of the city below him and laved it in a flood of romance and glamour. Most of Quotz was unlighted, for the streets had no lamps and the windows were shut up tight against thieves, vampires and demons. Occasionally the torchflares of the servants of a drunken noble or rich man moved down the dark canyons between the towering overhanging houses.

Beyond the city was the amphitheater formed by the hills curving out to the north and the great brick wall built to continue the natural windbreak. A wide opening had been left so that the 'rollers, their sails furled, could be towed in or out. Past this the great plain suddenly began, as if the hand of some immense landscaper had pressed the hills flat and declared that from here on there would be no uneven-nesses.

Westward lay the incredibly level stretch of the grassy ground of the Xurdimur. Ten thousand miles straight across, flat as a table top, broken only here and there by clumps of forests, ruins of cities, waterholes, the tents of the no-madic savages, herds of wild animals, packs of grass cats and dire dogs, and the mysterious and undoubtedly imag-inary "roaming islands," great clumps of rock and dirt that legend said slid of their own volition over the plains. How like this planet, he thought, that the greatest peril to navi-gation should be one that existed only in the heads of the inhabitants.

The Xurdimur was a fabulous phenomenon, without par-allel. On none of the many planets that Earthmen had dis-covered was there anything similar. How, he wondered, could the plain keep its smoothness, when there was always dirt running on to it from the eroding hills and mountains that ringed it? The rains, too, should have done much to wear it away unevenly. Of course, the grass that grew all over it was long and had very tough roots. And if what he had been told was true, beneath the vegetation was one mass of inextricably tangled roots that held the soil together.

There was another thing to consider, though: the winds that blew all the way across the Xurdimur and furnished propulsion for the wheeled sailing craft. To have winds you must have pressure differentials, which were usually caused by heat differentials. Although the Xurdimur was ringed by mountains there were no large eminences on it for ten thousand miles, nothing to replenish the currents of air. Or so it seemed to his limited knowledge of meteorology, though he did wonder how the trade winds that swept Earth's seas managed to keep going for so many thousands of leagues, just on their original impetus. Or did they get boosts? He didn't know.

What he did know was that the Xurdimur was a thing that shouldn't be. Yet, the very presence of men here was just as amazing, just as preposterous. Homo sapiens was scattered throughout the Galaxy. Everywhere that the space-traveling Earthmen had gone, they had found that about every fourth inhabitable planet was populated by men of their species. The proof lay not just in the outward physical resemblance of terrestrial and extra-terrestrial; it lay in their ability to breed. Earthmen, Sirian, Albirean, Vegan, it made no difference. Their men could have children by the women of other planets.

Naturally there had been many theories to account for this fact. All had as a common basis the assumption that Homo sapiens had sometime, somewhere, in the very remote past, originated on one planet and then had spread out over the Galaxy from it. And, somehow, space travel had been lost and each race had gone back to savagery, only to begin again the long hard struggle toward civilization and the rediscovery of spaceships. Why, no one knew. One could only guess.

There was the problem of language. It might seem that if man had come from a common birthplace he would at least have kept a trace of his home language and that the linguists could break down the development of tongue and link one planet to another through it. But no. Every world had its own Tower of Babel, its own ten thousand languages. The terrestrial scientist might trace Russian and English and Swedish, and Lithuanian and Persian and Hindustani back to a proto-Indo-European, but he had never found on any other planet a language which he could say had also derived from the Aryan Ursprache.

Green's mind wandered to the two Earthmen now imprisoned in the city of Estorya. He hoped they weren't being treated badly. They could be in horrible pain at this very moment, if the priests felt like subjecting them to a little demon-testing.

Thinking of torture led him to sit up a little straighter and to stretch his arms and legs. In an hour he was supposed to meet the Duchess. To do that he had to go through the supposedly secret door in the wall of the turret at the northern end of the walk, up a stairway through a passage between the walls, and so to the Duchess's apartments. There one of the maids-of-honor would usher him into Zuni's presence and then would try to eavesdrop so she could report to the Duke later on. Zuni and Green weren't supposed to know about this, but were to pretend that she was their trusted confidante.

When the great bell of the Temple of the God of Time, Grooza, struck, Green would rise from his bench and go to what he now thought of as a wearisome chore. If that woman could only be interested in talking of something else besides her complexion or digestion, or idle palace gossip, it wouldn't be so bad. But no, she chattered on and on, and Green would get increasingly sleepy, yet would not dare drop off for fear of irreparably offending her. And to do that . . .

7

THE LESSER MOON had touched the western horizon and the greater was nearing the zenith when Green awoke and jumped to his feet, swearing in sheer terror. He'd fallen asleep and kept Zuni waiting.

"My God, what'll she say?" he said aloud. "What'll I tell her?"

"You needn't tell me anything," came her angry retort from very close by. He started, and whirled around and saw that she'd been standing behind him. She was wrapped in a robe, but her pale face gleamed from beneath the overhanging hood and her mouth was opened. White teeth flashed as she began accusing him of not loving her, of being bored by her, of loving some other woman, probably a slave girl, a good-for-nothing, lazy, brainless, emptily pretty wench.

If his situation hadn't been so serious Green would have smiled at her self-portrayal.

He tried to dam the flood, but to no avail. She screeched at him to shut up, and when he put his fingers to his lips and said, "Shhh!" she replied by raising her voice even more.

"You know you're not supposed to be out of your rooms after dark unless the Duke is along," he said, taking her elbow and attempting to steer her down the walk toward the secret door. "If the guards see you there'll be trouble, bad trouble. Let's go."

Unfortunately the guards did see them. Torches appeared at the foot of the steps below the walk, and iron helmets and cuirasses gleamed. Green tried to urge her on faster, for there was still time to make it to the door. She jerked her arm loose and shouted, "Take your filthy hands off me, you Northern slave! The Duchess of Tropat doesn't allow herself to be pushed around by a blond beast!"

"Damn it," he snarled, and he shoved her. "You stupid *kizmaiaz!* Get going! *You* won't be tortured if they find us together!"

Zuni jerked away. Her face twisted and her mouth worked soundlessly. *"Kizmaiaz!"* she finally gasped. *"Kizmaiaz* yourself!"

Suddenly she began screaming. Before he could clamp his hand over her mouth, she dashed past him and toward the steps. It was then that he came out of his paralysis and ran, not after her, which he knew was useless, but toward the secret door. All was up. It was absolutely no use trying to explain to the guards. The situation had now entered a conventional phase. She would tell the guards that he had come into her room, through some unknown means—which would be "found out" later—and had dragged her out onto the walk, apparently with the intention of violating her. Why he should pick a public place when he already had the privacy of her rooms would not be asked. And the guards, though they would know what really had happened, would pretend to believe her and would furiously seize him and drag him off to the dungeons. The absurd thing about it was that within a few days the whole city, including Zuni herself, would believe that her story was true. By the time he'd been executed they would hate his guts, and the lot of all the slaves would be miserable for a while because they would share his blame.

Green had no intention of being seized. Flight was an admission of guilt, but it made no difference now.

He ran through the secret door, shut and bolted it and raced up the steps that led to her apartments. The guards would have to take the long way around; he had at least two minutes before they could unlock the two doors of the anterooms to her quarters, explain to the guards just outside them what had happened and begin a search for him. As for him, he was running like a rabbit, but he was thinking like a fox. Having known that just such a situation might arise, he had long ago planned in detail several possible courses of action. Now, he chose the likeliest one and began acting efficiently—if not smoothly.

The staircase was a narrow corkscrew with room for only one person at a time to go up. He ran up it so fast that he got dizzy with the ever-winding turns. He reeled and had trouble keeping from falling to his left when he did arrive at its top. Nevertheless he did not pause to catch breath or balance but pulled the lever that would make the door swing out. He burst through it. No one there, thank God. He stopped for a moment, listened to make sure nobody was in the next room, then pushed on a boss set in a pattern of bronze protuberances, which was connected with the mechanism that operated the secret door. The section of wall swung back silently until it was flush with the rest, and quite indistinguishable. He then twisted the knob so the door couldn't be opened from the other side. Green took time to give fervent thanks to the builders of the castle, who had prepared this device for the owners to hide within in case of a successful invasion or revolt. If it had not been there he could not have escaped.

Escaped? He'd only put off his inevitable capture. But he intended to run as long as he could and then fight until they were forced to kill him.

The first thing to do was to find a weapon. As a matter of fact, he was so familiar with Zuni's rooms that he knew exactly where he could get what he wanted. He walked through two large rooms, making his way easily even through the feeble duskish light that the few oil lamps and candles furnished. Hanging from the wall of the third room was a saber made of the best steel obtainable on this planet and fashioned by the greatest smiths, the swordwrights of far-away and almost legendary Talamasko. The blade was a gift from Zuni's father on the occasion of her wedding to the Duke. It was supposed to be given by Zuni to her eldest son when he came of weapon-carrying age. The hilt had a guard on which was inscribed in gold the motto: *Sooner hell than dishonor*. He fastened sword and scabbard to an iron ring on his broad leather belt, went to a luxurious dressing table, pulled open a drawer and took out a stiletto. This he stuck through his belt, also a huge flintlock pistol with a gold-and-ivory chased butt. He loaded it with powder and an iron ball he found in a compartment and put ammunition in a bag, which he also hung from his belt. Then, well armed, he walked out onto the balcony to take a quick view of the situation.

Three stories below him was the walk which he had left a few minutes before. Many soldiers, and Zuni, were standing there, all looking up. As his face came into sight, visible in the moonlight and the up-reaching flares of their torches, a shout arose. Several of the musket men raised their long-barreled weapons, but Zuni cried out for them to hold their fire, she wanted him alive. Green's skin prickled at the vindictiveness in her voice and at the vision of what she was probably planning for him. He'd been forced to see too many tortures and public executions not to know exactly what she designed for him. Suddenly overcome with rage that she could be so treacherous and brutal, a rage perhaps flavored with self-disgust because he had made love to her, he aimed his pistol at her. There was a click as the hammer struck the flint, a spark, a whoosh as the powder burnt in the pan, a loud bang and a cloud of black smoke. When the fumes cleared away, he saw that everybody, including the Duchess, was running for cover. Naturally, he'd missed, for he'd had almost no practice with the pistols, being a slave. Even if he'd been well trained, he probably would not have struck his mark, so inaccurate were the weapons.

While Green was reloading he heard a shout from above. Looking up, he saw the Duke's round face, pale in the moonlight, hanging over the railing of the balcony above. He raised his empty pistol, and the Duke, squalling with fear, ran back into his quarters. Green laughed and said to himself that even if he was killed now he would at least have the satisfaction of knowing that he had shamed the Duke, who was always boasting about his bravery in battle. Of course, his action had also made it absolutely necessary for the Duke to have him killed at once, so that Green could not tell others that he'd put him to flight.

He grinned crookedly. What would happen when the soldiers received the Duke's orders, directly contradicting the Duchess's? The poor fellows would scarcely know what to do. The man's commands would of course supersede the woman's. But the woman would be furious and she would later on find some means of punishing those who did succeed in killing Green.

It was at that moment that he lost his smile and paled with fright. A loud deep-chested barking nearby. Not outside the apartment's door, but *inside!*

He cursed and whirled around just in time to see the large body launched toward his throat, the white fangs flashing and the green fire shining from its eyes as the moonlight struck them.

Even in that moment of panic he realized that he'd forgotten the small door set inside the larger one so that Alzo could have admittance at any time. And if the big dog could get through, then soldiers could also crawl through!

Instinctively he thrust out the pistol and squeezed the trigger. It did not go off, for there was no powder in the pan. But the barrel did jam into the great mouth and deflect Alzo from his target, Green's throat. Even so, Green was knocked backward by the impact, and he felt the sharp teeth clamping down on his wrist. Those jaws were capable of biting through his arm, and though he felt no pain, he was sickened by the thought that he'd see a bloody stump when Alzo danced away from him. However, his arm, though dripping blood from large gashes, was not hurt badly. The dog had been deterred by the barrel shoved down his throat, choking him so that he could think of nothing for the moment but getting clear of it.

The pistol clattered on the iron floor of the balcony. Alzo shook his head, unaware in his frenzy that he was rid of the weapon. Green leaped up from the sitting position into which Alzo's charge had flung him against the railing. Snarling as viciously as the dog, he braced his feet against the juncture of the floor and railing and launched himself straight out. At the same time, the canine jumped. They met head on, Green's skull driving into the open mouth and knocking the dog backward because his impetus was greater. Though the huge jaws bit down at his scalp, they snapped on air, and the animal fell to one side, growling. Green seized hold of the long tail, rolled away from the teeth now snapping at his ankles, and jerked at the tail so that the dog would swing away from him. He rose to one knee, pushed the dog away from him, though still keeping his frenzied grip with two hands, and jumped to his feet. Frantically, the animal twisted around and bit at the imprisoning hands. But he succeeded only in biting his own flank. Howling in anguish, he tried to lunge away. Green, making a supreme effort, raised the tail in the air. Naturally, the body came with it. At the same time he half-turned from the animal, bent forward and, with a convulsive motion, using his bowed back as a lever, threw Alzo over his head.

8

THE TERRIBLE GROWLING suddenly changed to a high-pitched howl of despair as Alzo flew over the railing and out into the air above the walk. Green, leaning over to watch him, did not feel sorry for him. He was exultant. He'd hated that dog and had dreamed of just such a moment.

Alzo's yelping was cut off as he struck the parapet beside the walk, bounced off, and then dropped from view into the depths beyond. Green's strength had been greater than he'd suspected, for he had thought only to toss the one hundred and fifty pound beast over the railing.

There was no time for savoring triumph. If the dog could get through that little door, so could soldiers. He ran out into the room, expecting that at least a dozen men had crawled in. But there was no one. Why? The only thing he could think of was that they were afraid, knowing that if he at once dispatched the dog, he could leisurely knock them over the head in their helpless on-all-fours position.

The door shook beneath a mighty impact. They'd taken the wiser, if the less courageous, course of battering rams. Green loaded his pistol, spilling the powder at his first attempt to prime the pan because his hands shook so. He fired, and a large hole appeared in the wood. However, part of the ball also stuck out, for the door was planked thickly against just such weapons.

The battering ceased and he heard a thud as the ram was dropped on the floor in hasty retreat. He smiled. As they were still operating under the Duchess's instructions to take him alive—not yet countermanded by the Duke's—they would not want to face pistol fire with only swords in hand. And in the first reflex to the shot they'd undoubtedly forgotten that a ball couldn't penetrate the wood.

"This is living!" said Green out loud. And he wondered that his voice shook as much as his legs did, and yet he felt a wild exultance shooting through his fear and knew that he was tasting both with a fine liking. Perhaps, he thought, he really liked this moment—even if his death was around the corner—because he'd been repressed so long and violence was a wonderful therapy for releasing his resentment and clamped-down-on fury. Whatever the reason, he knew that this was one of the high moments of his life and that if he survived he'd look back on it with pleasure and pride. And that was the strangest thing of all, since in his culture the young were taught to abhor violence. Luckily, they weren't so conditioned against it that the very thought of it paralyzed them. No hard neural paths had been set up against the action of violence; it was just that, philosophically speaking, they loathed the concept. Fortunately, there was a philosophy of the body, too, a much older and deeper one. And while it was true that man could no more live without philosophy of the mind than he could without bread, it had no place in Green at present. The fiery breath that flooded his body now and made him so sensitive to what a fine thing it was to be alive while death was knocking at the door did not rise from any mental abstraction or profound meditation.

Green rolled back the carpets that led from the room to the balcony, for he wanted a firm footing if it became necessary to make a running broad jump from the balcony in an effort to clear the walk below and drop into the moat. He'd have to have very good timing and do everything just right the first time, like a parachute jump, otherwise he'd end up with broken bones on the hard stones below.

Not that he was going to make that leap unless he just had to. But he was leaving an avenue open if his other measures didn't work.

Again he ran to the bureau and drew out a large bag of gunpowder, weighing at least five pounds. In the open end of this he inserted a fuse, and tied the neck around it. While he was doing this, he heard shouts and cheers as the soldiers returned to the door, picked up their ram and hurled themselves at the thick planking. He did not bother shooting again but instead lit the fuse with a candle. Then he walked to the large door, pushed out the small dog's door and tossed the bag through it. He jumped back and ran, though there was little chance that the resultant explosion would harm the door.

There was a silence as the soldiers were probably staring paralyzed at the smoking fuse. Then—a roar! The room shook, the door fell in, blasted off its hinges, and black smoke poured in. Green ran into the cloud, got down on all fours, scuttled through the doorway, cursed desperately when the hilt of his sword caught on the doorframe, tore loose and lunged through into the dense smoke that filled the anteroom. His groping hands felt the ram where it had dropped, and the wet warm face of a soldier who'd fallen.

He coughed sharply from the biting fumes but went on until his head butted into the wall. Then he felt to his right, where he imagined the door was, came to it, passed through and on into the next room, also filled with a cloud. After he'd scuttled like a bug across its floor, he dared to open his eyes for a quick look. The smoke was thinner and was pouring out the door to the hallway, just in front of him. He saw no feet in the clearer area between the floor and the bottom of the clouds, so he rose and walked through the door. To his left, he knew, the hall led to a stairway that was probably now jammed with soldiers. To his right would be another stairway that went up to the Duke's apartments. That was the only way he could go.

Luckily the smoke was still so dense in the corridor that those assembled on the left staircase couldn't see him. They'd think he was in the Duchess's rooms yet, and he hoped that when they did rush it and didn't find him there the rolled-back carpets would give them the idea that he'd taken a running broad jump from the balcony. In which case, they'd at once search the moat for him. And if they didn't find him swimming there, as they wouldn't, then they might presume he'd either drowned or else got to the shore and was now somewhere in the darkness of the city.

He felt along the wall toward the staircase, his other hand gripping the stiletto. When his fingers ran across the arm of a man leaning against the wall, he withdrew them at once, bent his knees and in a crouching position ran in the general direction of the stairs. The smoke got even thinner here so that he saw the steps in time to avoid falling over them. Unfortunately the Duke and another man were also there. Both saw his figure emerge into the torchlight from the clouds, but he had the advantage of knowing who he was, so that he had plunged the thin stiletto into the soldier's throat before he could act. The Duke tried to leap past Green, but the Earthman stuck a leg out and tripped him. Then he grabbed the ruler's arm, twisted it behind his back, forced him up and on his knees and, using the arm as a cruel lever, raised him. He enjoyed hearing the Duke moan, though he'd never consciously taken pleasure in pain before. He had time to think that perhaps he liked this because of the torture the Duke had inflicted on his many helpless victims. Of course, he, Green, a highly civilized man, shouldn't be feeling this way. But the rightness or wrongness of an emotion never kept anybody from experiencing it.

"Up you go!" he said in a low, harsh voice, directing the Duke toward his apartments, manipulating the twisted arm as a steering column. By then the smoke had cleared away so that those at the other end of the corridor could see that something was wrong. A shout arose, followed by the slap of running feet on the stone flags. Green stopped, turned the Duke so he faced the approaching crowd and said to him, "Tell them that I will kill you unless they go away."

To emphasize his point he stuck the end of the stiletto into the Duke's back and pressed hard enough to draw blood. The Duke quivered, then became rigid. Nevertheless he said, "I will not do so. That would be dishonor."

Green couldn't help admiring such courage, even if it did make his predicament worse. He refused to kill the Duke just then because that would throw away the only trump card he held at that moment. So he stuck the stiletto in his teeth and, still holding with one hand to the Duke's twisted arm, took the Duke's pistol from his belt and fired over his shoulder.

There was a whoosh of flame that burned the Duke's ear and made him give a cry that was almost drowned out in the roar of the explosion. The nearest man threw up his hands, dropping his spear, and fell on his face. The others stopped. Doubtless, they were still operating under the Duchess's orders not to kill Green, for the Duke must have arrived at the foot of the staircase just in time to witness the explosion of the gunpowder. And he was in no condition to issue contrary orders, being deafened and stunned by the report almost going off in his ear.

Green shouted out, "Go back, or I will kill the Duke! It is his wish that you go back to the stairs and do not bother us until he sends word to you!"

By the flickering light of the torches he could see the puzzled expression on the soldiers' faces. It was only then he realized that in his extreme excitement he had shouted the orders in English. Hastily, he translated his demands, and was relieved to see them turn and retreat, though reluctantly. He then half-dragged the Duke up the steps to his apartments, where he barred the door and primed his pistol again.

"So far, so good!" he said in English. "The question is what now, little man?"

The ruler's rooms were even more luxurious than his wife's, and were larger because they had to contain not only the Duke's hundreds of hunting trophies, including human heads, but his collection of glass birds. Indeed, one might easily see where his heart really lay, for the heads had collected dust, whereas each and every glittering winged creature was immaculate. It would have gone hard on a servant who'd neglected his cleaning duties in the great rooms dedicated to the collection.

On seeing them Green smiled slightly.

When you're fighting for your life, hit a man where he's softest. . . .

9

It was a matter of two minutes to tie the Duke in a chair with several of the hunting whips hanging from the walls.

Meanwhile the Duke came out of his daze. He began screaming every invective he knew—and he knew quite a lot—and promising every refined torture he could think of—and his knowledge was not poverty-stricken in that area either. Green waited until the Duke had given himself a bad case of laryngitis. Then he told him, in a firm but quiet voice, what he intended to do unless the Duke got him out of the castle. To emphasize his determination, he picked up a bludgeon studded with iron spikes and swung it whistling through the air. The Duke's eyes widened, and he paled. All of a sudden he changed from a defiant ruler challenging his captor to inflict his worst upon him to a shrunken, trembling old man.

"And I will smash every last bird in these rooms," said Green. "And I will open the chest that lies behind that pile of furs and take out of it your most precious treasure, the bird you have not even shown to the Emperor for fear he would get jealous and demand it as a gift from you, the bird you take out at rare intervals and over which you gloat all night."

"My wife told you!" gasped the Duke. "Oh, what an *izzot* she is!"

"Granted," said Green. "She babbled to me many secrets, being a featherbrained, idle, silly, stupid female, a fit consort for you. So I know where the unique *exurotr* statuette made by Izan Yushwa of Metzva Moosh is hidden, the glass bird that cost the whole dukedom a great tax and brought many bitter tears and hardships from your subjects. I will have no compunction about destroying it even if it is the only one ever made and if Izan Yushwa is now dead so that it can never be replaced."

The Duke's eyes bulged in horror.

"No, no!" he said in a quavering voice. "That would be unthinkable, blasphemous, sacrilegious! Have you no sense of beauty, degenerate slave that you are, that you would smash forever that most beautiful of all things made by the hands of man?"

"I would."

The Duke's mouth drew down at the corners; suddenly, he was weeping.

Green was embarrassed, for he knew how great must be the emotion that could make this man, educated in a hard school, break down before an enemy. And he reflected upon what a strange thing a human being was. Here was a man who would literally allow his throat to be cut before he would display cowardice by bargaining for it. But to have his precious collection of glass birds threatened...!

Green shrugged. Why try to understand it? The only thing

to do was to use whatever came his way.

"Very well, if you wish to save them you must do this." And he detailed exactly the Duke's moves and orders for the next ten minutes. He thereupon made him swear by the most holy oaths and upon his family name and by the honor of the founder of his family that he would not betray Green.

"To make sure," added the Earthman, "I shall take the *exurotr* with me. Once I know your word is good I'll take steps to see that it is returned undamaged to you."

"Can I depend on that?" breathed the Duke hoarsely, rolling his big brown eyes.

"Yes, I will contact Zingaro, Business Agent of the Thieves' Guild, and he will return it to you, for a compensation, of course. But before we conclude this bargain you must swear that you will not harm Amra, my wife, nor any of her children, nor confiscate her business but will behave toward her as if this had never happened."

The Duke swallowed hard, but he swore. Green was happy, because, though he was going to desert Amra, he was at least insuring her future.

It was a long, long hour later that Green came out of his hiding place inside a large closet in the Duke's apartment. Even though the Duke had sworn the holiest of oaths, he was as treacherous as any of the barbarians on this planet, and that was very treacherous indeed. Green had stood behind the door, sweating and listening to the loud and sometimes incoherent conversation taking place between the Duke, his soldiers and the Duchess. The Duke was a good actor, for he convinced everybody that he had escaped from the mad slave Green, had seized a sword and forced him to make a running broad jump from the balcony railing. Of course, several guardsmen had seen a large man-sized object hurtle from the balcony and fall with a loud splash into the moat below. There was no doubt that the slave must have broken his back when he struck the water or else he had been knocked out and then drowned. Whatever had happened, he had not come out.

Green, his ear against the door, could not help smiling at this, despite his tension. He and the Duke had combined forces to heave out a wooden statue of the god Zuzupatr, weighted with iron dishes tied to it so that it wouldn't float. In the moonlight and the excitement, the idol must have looked enough like a falling man to deceive anybody.

The only one seemingly not satisfied was Zuni. She raised every kind of hell she knew, behaved in a most undignified manner, screeched at her husband because his blood-thirstiness and lack of restraint had robbed her of the exquisite tortures she'd planned for the slave who had attempted to dishonor her. The Duke, his face getting redder and redder, had suddenly bellowed out at her to quit acting like a condemned *izzot* and go at once to her apartments. To show that he meant what he said he ordered several soldiers to escort her. Zuni, however, was too stupid to see how perilous was her situation, how near the headsman's ax. She raved on until the Duke gave a sign and two soldiers seized her elbows—at least, Green supposed they did, for she yelled at them to take their dirty hands off her—and propelled her out of the rooms. Even then it took some time before the Duke could close the doors on his last guest.

The little ruler opened the door. In his hand he held a priest's green robe, the sacerdotal hexagonal spectacles and a mask for the lower part of the face. The mask was customarily worn when a monk was on a mission for a high dignitary. During the time the face was covered the monk was under a vow not to speak to anyone until he had reached the person for whom he had a message. Thus, Green would not be bothered with any embarrassing questions.

He put on the robe, spectacles and mask, threw the hood over his head and placed the glass *exurotr* inside his shirt.

His loaded pistol he kept up one capacious sleeve, holding it with the other hand.

"Remember," said the Duke anxiously as he opened the door and peered out to see if anybody was on the staircase, "remember that you must take every precaution against damaging the *exurotr*. Tell Zingaro that he must at once pack it in a chest filled with silks and sawdust so it won't break. I will die a thousand deaths until it comes back once again to my collection."

And I, thought Green, will die a thousand deaths until I get safely out of your reach, out of the city and far away on a windroller.

He promised again that he would keep his word as well as the Duke kept his, but that he would also take every measure to insure against treachery. Then he slipped out and closed the door. He was on his own until he boarded the *Bird of Fortune*.

10

HE HAD NO trouble at all, except for making his way through the thick traffic. The explosions and shouting coming from the castle had aroused the whole town, so that everybody who could stand on his two feet, or could get somebody to carry him, was outside, milling around, asking questions, talking excitedly and in general trying to make as much chaos as possible and to enjoy every bit of this excuse to take part in a general disturbance. Green strode through them, his head bent but his eyes probing ahead. He made fairly good progress, only being held up temporarily a few times by the human herd.

Finally the flat plain of the windbreak lay before him, and the many masts of the great wheeled vessels were a forest around him. He was able to get to the *Bird of Fortune* unchallenged by any of the dozens of guardsmen that he passed. The 'roller herself lay snugly between two docks, where a huge gang of slaves had towed her. There was a gangway running up from one of the docks, and at both ends stood a sailor on guard, clad in the family colors of yellow, violet and crimson. They chewed *grixtr* nut, something like betel except that it stained both teeth and lips and gave them a green color.

When Green stepped boldly upon the gangway the nearest guard looked doubtful and put his hand on his knife. Evidently he'd had no orders from Miran about a priest, but he knew what the mask indicated and that awed him enough so that he did not dare oppose the stranger. Nor was the second guard any quicker in making up his mind. Green slipped by him, entered the mid-decks and walked up the gangway to the foredeck. He knocked quietly on the door of the captain's cabin. A moment later it swung violently open; light flooded out, then was blocked off by Miran's huge round bulk.

Green stepped inside, pressing the captain back, Miran reached for his dagger but stopped when he saw the intruder take off the mask and spectacles and throw back the hood.

"Green! So you made it! I did not think it was possible."

"With me all things are possible," replied Green modestly. He sat down at the table, or rather crumpled at it, and began repeating in a dry voice, halting with fatigue, the story of his escape. In a few minutes the narrow cabin rang with the captain's laughter and his one eye twinkled and beamed as he slapped Green on the back and said that by all the gods here was a man he was proud to have aboard.

"Have a drink of this Lespaxian wine, even better than Chalousma, and one I bring out only for honored guests," said Miran, chortling.

Green reached out a hand for the proffered glass, but his fingers never closed upon the stem, for his head sank onto the tabletop, and his snores were tremendous.

• • •

It was three days later that a much-rested Green, his skin comfortably, even glowingly, tight with superb Lespaxian, sat at the table and waited for the word to come that he could finally leave the cabin. The first day of inactivity he'd slept and eaten and paced back and forth, anxious for news of what was going on in the city. At nightfall Miran had returned with the story that a furious search was organized in the city itself and the outlying hills. Of course, the Duke would insist that the 'rollers themselves be turned inside-out, and Miran was cursing because that would mean a fatal delay. They could not wait for more than three more days. The fish tanks had been installed; the provisions were almost all in the hold; his roistering crewmen were being dragged out of the taverns and sobered up; two days after tomorrow the great vessel would have to be towed out of the windbreak and sails set for the perilous and long voyage.

"I wouldn't worry," said Green. "You will find that to-morrow word will come from the hills that Green has been killed by a wild man of the Clan Axaquexcan, who will demand money before handling the dead slave's head over. The Duke will accept this as true and will conveniently forget all about searching the 'rollers."

Miran rubbed his fat oily palms, while one pale eye glowed. He loved a good intrigue, the more elaborate the better.

But the second day, even though what Green had predicted came true Miran became nervous and began to find the big blond man's constant presence in his cabin irksome. He wanted to send him down into the hold, but Green firmly refused, reminding the captain of his promise of haven within these very walls. He then calmly appropriated another bottle of the merchant's Lespaxian, having located its hiding place, and drank it. Miran glowered, and his face twitched with repressed resentment, but he said nothing because of the custom that a guest could do what he pleased—within reasonable limits.

The third day Miran was positively a tub of nerves, jittery, sweating, pacing back and forth. At last he left the cabin, only to begin pacing back and forth on the deck. Green could hear his footsteps for hours. The fourth day he was up at dawn and bellowing orders to his crewmen. A little later Green felt the big vessel move and heard the shouts of the foremen of the towing gangs and the chants of the slaves as they bent their backs hauling at the huge ropes attached to the 'roller.

Slowly, oh, so slowly it seemed to Green, the craft creaked forward. He dared open a curtain to look out the square porthole. Before him was the rearing side of another 'roller, and just for a second it seemed to him that it, not his vessel, was the one that was moving. Then he saw that the 'roller was advancing at a pace of about fifteen or sixteen feet a minute. It would take them an hour to get past the towering brick walls of the windbreak.

He sweated out that hour and unconsciously fell into his childhood habit of biting his nails, expecting at any time to see the docks suddenly boil with soldiers running after the *Bird of Fortune*, shouting for it to stop because it had a runaway slave aboard.

But no such thing occurred, and at last the tug gangs stopped and began coiling up their ropes, and Green quit chewing his nails. Miran shouted orders, the first mate repeated them, there was the slap of many feet on the decks above, the sound of many voices chanting. A sound as of a knife cutting cloth told that the sails had been released. Suddenly, the vessel rocked as the wind caught it and a vibration through the floors announced that the big axles were turning, the huge wheels with their tires of *chacorotr*, a kind of rubber, were revolving. The *Bird* was on the wing!

Green opened the door slightly and took one last look at

the city of Quotz. It was receding rapidly at the rate of fifteen miles an hour, and at this distance it looked like a toy city nestled in the lap of a hillock. Now that the danger from it was gone and the odors too far away to offend his nose it looked quite romantic and enticing.

"And so we say farewell to exotic Quotz," murmured Green in the approved travelog fashion. "So long, you son of an *izzot!*"

Then, though he was supposed to stay inside until Miran summoned him, he opened the door and stepped out.

And almost fainted dead away.

"Hello, honey," said Amra.

Green scarcely heard the children grouped around her also extend their greetings. He was just coming out of the dizziness and blackness that had threatened to overcome him. Perhaps it was the wine coupled with the shock. Perhaps, he was to think later, it was just that he was plain scared, scared as he'd not been in the castle. Ashamed, too, that Amra had found out his plans to desert her, and deeply ashamed because she loved him anyway and would not allow him to go without her. She had a tremendous pride that must have cost her great effort to choke down.

Probably, he was to say to himself later on, it was sheer fear of her tongue that made him quail so. There was nothing that a man dreaded so much as a woman's tonguelashing, especially if he deserved it. Oh, especially!

That was to come later. At the moment Amra was strangely quiet and meek. All she would say was that she had many business connections and that she knew well Zingaro, the Thieves' Guild Business Agent. They had been childhood playmates, and they'd helped each other in various shady transactions since. It was only natural that she should hear about the *exurotr* a slave hiding on the *Bird of Fortune* had given Zingaro to take back to the Duke. Cornering Zingaro, she had worked out of him enough information to be sure that Green had escaped to the 'roller. After all, Zingaro was under oath only to be reticent about certain details of the whole matter. From there she had taken the business into her own hands, had told Miran that she would inform the Duchess of Green's whereabouts unless he permitted her and her family to go along on the voyage.

"Here I am, your faithful and loyal wife," she said, opening her arms in an expansive gesture.

"I am overwhelmed with emotion," replied Green, for once not exaggerating.

"Then come and embrace me," she cried, "and don't stand there as if you'd seen the dead return from the grave!"

"Before all these people?" he said, half-stunned, looking around at the grinning captain and first mate on the foredeck beside him and at the sailors and their families on the mid-deck below. The only ones not watching him were the goggled helmsmen, whose backs were turned because they were intent on wrestling with the great spoked wheel.

"Why not?" she retorted. "You'll be sleeping on the open deck with them, eating with them, breathing their breath, feeling their elbows at every turn, cursing, laughing, fighting, getting drunk, making love, all, all on the open deck. So why not embrace me? Or don't you want me to be here?"

"The thought never entered my head," he said, stepping up to her and taking her in his arms. Or, if it had, he reflected, you can bet that I'd not dare say it.

After all, it was good to feel her soft, warm, firmly curved body again and know that there was at least one person on this godforsaken planet that cared for him. What could have made him think for one minute that he could endure life without her?

Well, he had. She just would not, could not, fit into his life if he ever got back on Earth.

11

MIRAN COUGHED and said, "You two and your children and maid must get off the deck and go to amidships. That is where you will live. Never again must you set foot upon the steering deck unless you are summoned. I run a tight ship and discipline is strictly adhered to."

Green followed Amra and the children down the steps to the deck below, noticing for the first time that Inzax, the pretty blond slave who took care of the children, was also aboard. You had to give credit to Amra. Wherever she went she traveled in style.

He also thought that if this was a tight ship a loose one must be sheer chaos. Cats and dogs were running here and there, playing with the many infants, or else fighting with each other. Women sat and sewed or hung up washing or dried dishes or nursed babies. Hens clucked defiantly from behind the bars of their coops, scattered everywhere. On the port side there was even a pigpen holding about thirty of the tiny rabbit-eared porcines.

Green followed Amra to a place where an awning had been stretched to make a roof

"Isn't this nice?" she said. "It has sides which we can pull down when it rains or when we want privacy, as I suppose we will, you being so funny in some ways."

"Oh, it's delightful," he hastened to assure her. "I see you even have some feather mattresses. And a cookstove."

He looked around. "But where are the fish tanks? I thought Miran was going to bolt them to the deck?"

"Oh, no, he said that they were too valuable to expose to gunfire if we encountered pirates. So he had the deck cut open wide enough to lower the tanks inside the hold. Then the deck planking was replaced. Most of these people here would be sleeping below if it weren't for the tanks. But there's no room now."

Green decided to take a look around. He liked to have a thorough knowledge of his immediate environment so that he would know how to behave if an emergency arose.

The windroller itself was about two hundred feet long. Its beam was about thirty-four feet. The hull was boat-shaped, and the narrow keel rested on fourteen axles. Twenty-eight enormous solid rubber-tired wheels turned at the ends of these axles. Thick ropes of the tough rubber-like substance were tied to the ends of the axles and to the tops of the hull itself. These were to hold the body steady and keep it from going over when the 'roller reeled under too strong a side wind and also to provide some resiliency when the 'roller was making a turn. Being aboard at such times was almost like being on a water-sailing ship. As the front pair of wheels—the steering wheels—turned and the longitudinal axis of the craft slowly changed direction, the body of the vessel, thrust by the shifting impact of the winds, also tilted. Not too far, never as far as a boat in similar case, but enough to give one an uneasy feeling. The cables on the opposing side would stretch to a degree and then would stop the sidewise motion of the keel and there would be a slight and slow roll to the other direction. Then a shorter and slower motion back again. It was enough to make a novice green. 'Roller sickness wasn't uncommon at the beginning of a voyage or during a violent windstorm. Like its aqueous counterpart, it affected the sufferer so that he could only hang over the rail and wish he *would* die.

The *Bird of Fortune* sported a curving bow and a high foredeck. On this was fastened the many-spoked steering wheel. Two helmsmen always attended it, two men wearing hexagonal goggles and close-fitting leather helmets with high crests of curled wire. Behind them stood the captain and first mate, giving their attention alternately to the helmsmen and to the sailors on deck and aloft. The middeck was sunken, and the poopdeck, though raised, was not as high as the foredeck.

The four masts were tall, but not as tall as those of a marine craft of similar size. High masts would have given the 'roller a tendency to capsize in a very strong wind, despite the weight of the axles and wheels. Therefore, the yardarms, reaching far out beyond the sides of the hull, were comparatively longer than a seaship's. When the *Bird* carried a full weight of canvas she looked, to a mariner's eyes, squat and ungainly. Moreover, yards had been fixed at right angles to the top of the hull and to the keel itself. Extra canvas was hung between these spars. The sight of all that sail sticking from between the wheels was enough to drive an old sailor to drink.

Three masts were square-rigged. The aft mast was fore-and-aft rigged and was used to help the steering. There was no bowsprit.

Altogether, it was a strange-looking craft. But once one

was accustomed to it, one saw it was as beautiful as a ship of the sea.

It was as formidable, too, for the *Bird* carried five large cannon on the middeck, six cannon on the second deck, a lighter swivel cannon the steering deck, and two swivels on the poopdeck.

Hung from davits were two long liferollers and a gig, all wheeled and with folding masts. If the *Bird* was wrecked it could be abandoned and all the crew could scoot off in the little rollers.

Green wasn't given much time for inspection. He became aware that a tall, lean sailor was regarding him intently. This fellow was dark-skinned but had the pale blue eyes of the Tropat hillsmen. He moved like a cat and wore a long, thin dagger, sharp as a claw. A nasty customer, thought Green.

Presently, the nasty customer, seeing that Green was not going to notice him, walked in front of him so that he could not help being annoyed. At the same time, the babble around them died and everybody turned his head to stare.

"Friend," said Green, affably enough, "would you mind standing off to one side? You are blocking my view."

The fellow spat *grixtr* juice at Green's feet.

"No slave calls me friend. Yes, I am blocking your view, and I would mind getting out of the way."

"Evidently you object to my presence here," said Green. "What is the matter? You don't like my face?"

"No, I don't. And I don't like to have as a crewmate a stinking slave."

"Speaking of odors," said Green, "would you please stand to leeward of me? I've been through a lot lately and I've a delicate stomach."

"Silence, you son of an *izzot!*" roared the sailor, red-faced. "Have respect toward your betters, or I'll strike you down and throw your body overboard."

"It takes two to make a murder, just as it takes two to make a bargain," said Green in a loud voice, hoping that Miran would hear and be reminded of his promise of protection. But Miran shrugged his shoulders. He had done as much as he could. It was up to Green to make his way from now on.

"It is true that I am a slave," he said. "But I was not born one. Before being captured I was a freeman who knew liberty as none of you here know it. I came from a country where there were no masters because every man was his own master.

"However, that is neither here nor there. The point is that I earned my freedom, that I fought like a warrior, not a slave, to get aboard the *Bird*. I wish to become a crew member, to become a blood-brother to the Clan Effenycan."

"Ah, indeed, and what can you contribute to the Clan that we should consider you worthy of sharing our blood?"

What indeed? Green thought. The sweat broke out all over his body, though the morning wind was cool.

At that moment he saw Miran speak to a sailor, who disappeared below decks and come out almost at once carrying a small harp in his hand. Oh, yes, now he remembered that he had told the captain what a wonderful harpist and singer he was, just the man that the Clan, eager for entertainment on the long voyages, would be likely to initiate.

The unfortunate thing about that was that Green couldn't play a note.

Nevertheless he took the instrument from the sailor and gravely plucked its strings. He listened to the tones, frowned, adjusted the pegs, plucked them again, then handed the harp back.

"Sorry, this is an inferior instrument," he said haughtily. "Haven't you anything better? I couldn't think of degrading my art on such a cheap monstrosity."

"Gods above!" screamed a man standing nearby. "That

is my harp you are talking about, the beloved harp of me, the bard Grazoot! Slave! Tone-deaf son of a laryngiteal mother! You will answer to me for that insult!"

"No," said the sailor, "this is my affair. I, Ezkr, will test this lubber's fitness to join the Clan and be called brother."

"Over my dead body, brother!"

"If you so wish it, brother!"

There were more angry words until presently Miran himself came down to the middeck. "By Mennirox, this is a disgrace!" he bellowed. "Two Effenycan quarreling before a slave! Come, make a decision quietly, or I will have you both thrown overboard. It is not too far to walk back to Quotz."

"We will cast dice to see who is the lucky man," said the sailor, Ezkr. Grinning gap-toothedly, he reached into the pouch that hung from his belt, and pulled out the hexagonal ivories. A few minutes later he rose from his knees, having won four out of six throws. Green was disappointed more than he cared to show, for he had hoped that if he had to fight anybody it would be the pudgy, soft-looking harpist, not the tough sailor.

Ezkr seemed to agree with Green that he could not have had worse luck. Chewing *grixtr* so rapidly that the green-flecked slaver ran down his long chin, Ezkr announced the terms that the blond slave would have to meet to prove his fitness.

12

FOR A MOMENT Green thought of leaving the ship and making his way on foot.

Miran protested loudly. "This is ridiculous. Why can you not fight on deck like two ordinary men and be satisfied if one gives the other a flesh wound? That way I won't stand the chance of losing you, Ezkr, one of my top topmen. If you should slip, who could take your place? This green hand here?"

Ezkr ignored his captain's indignation, knowing that the code of the Clan protected him. He spit and said, "Anybody can wield a dagger. I want to see what kind of a man this Green is aloft. Walking a yard is the best way to see the color of his blood."

Yes, thought Green, his skin goose-pimpling. You'll likely see my blood all right, splashed from here to the horizon when I fall!

He asked Miran if he could withdraw a moment to his tent to pray to his gods for success. Miran nodded, and Green had Amra let down the sides of his shelter while he dropped to his knees. As soon as his privacy was assured, he handed her a long turban cloth and told her to go outside. She looked surprised, but when he told her what else she was to do, she smiled and kissed him.

"You are a clever man, Alan. I was right to prefer you above any other man I might have had, and I could have had the best."

"Save the compliments for afterwards, when we'll know if it works," he said. "Hurry to the stove and do what I say. If anybody asks you what you are up to, tell them that the stuff is necessary for my religious ritual. The gods," he said as she ducked through the tent opening, "often come in handy. If they didn't exist it would be necessary to invent them."

Amra paused and turned with an adoring face. "Ah, Alan, that is one of the many things for which I love you. You are always originating these witty sayings. How clever, and how dangerously blasphemous!"

He shrugged, airily dismissing her compliment as if it were nothing.

In a minute she returned with the turban wrapped around something limp but heavy. And within two minutes he stepped out from the tent, clad in a loincloth, leather belt, dagger and turban. Silently, be began climbing the rope ladder that rose to the tip of the nearest mast. Behind him came Ezkr.

He did get some encouragement from Amra and the children. The Duke's two boys cried out to him to cut the so-and-so's throat, but if he was killed instead, they would avenge him when they grew up, if not sooner. Even the blond maid, Inzax, wept. He felt somewhat better, for it was good to know that some people cared for him. And the knowledge that he had to survive and make sure that these women and children didn't come to grief was an added stimulus.

Nevertheless he felt his momentarily gained courage oozing out of his sweat pores with every step upward. It was so high up here, and so far down below. The craft itself became smaller and smaller and the people shrank to dolls, to upturned white faces that soon became less faces than blanks. The wind howled through the rigging and the mast, which had seemed so solid and steady when he was at its base, now became fragile and swaying.

"It takes guts to be a sailor and a blood-brother of the Clan Effenycan," said Ezkr. "Do you have them, Green?"

"Yes, but if I get any sicker I'll lose them, and you'll be sorry, being below me," muttered Green to himself.

Finally, after what seemed endless clambering into the very clouds themselves, he arrived at the topmost yard. If he had thought the mast thin and flexible, the arm seemed like a toothpick poised over an abyss. And he was supposed to inch his way out to the whipping tip, then turn and come back fighting!

"If you were not a coward you would stand up and walk out," called Ezkr.

"Sticks and stones will break my bones," replied Green, but did not enlighten the puzzled sailor as to what he meant. Sitting down on the yard, he put his legs around it and began working his way out. Halfway to the arm he stopped and dared to look down. Once was enough. There was nothing but hard, grassy ground directly beneath him, seemingly a mile below, and the flat plain rushing by, and the huge wheels turning, turning.

"Go on!" shouted Ezkr.

Green turned his head and told him in indelicate language what he could do with the yard and the whole ship for that matter if he could manage it.

Ezkr's dark face reddened and he stood up and began walking out on the yard. Green's eyes widened. This man could actually do it!

But when he was a few feet away the sailor stopped and said, "No, you are trying to anger me so I will grapple with you here and perhaps be pushed off, since you have a firmer hold. No, I will not be such a fool. It is you who must try to get past me."

He turned and walked almost carelessly back to the mast, against which he leaned while he waited.

"You have to go out to the very end," he repeated. "Else you won't pass the test even if you should get by me, which, of course, you won't."

Green gritted his teeth and humped out to what he considered close enough to the end, about two feet away. Any more might break the arm, as it was already bending far down. Or so it seemed to him.

He then backed away, managed to turn, and to work back to within several feet of Ezkr. Here he paused to regain his breath, his strength and his courage.

The sailor waited, one hand on a rope to steady himself, the other with its dagger held point-out at Green.

The Earthman began unwinding his turban. "What are you doing?" said Ezkr, frowing with sudden anxiety.

Up to this point he had been master, because he knew what to expect. But if something unconventional happened...

Green shrugged his shoulders and continued his very careful and slow unwrapping of his headpiece.

"I don't want to spill this," he said.

"Spill what?"

"This!" shouted Green, and he whipped the turban upward towards Ezkr's face.

The turban itself was too far from the sailor to touch him. But the sand contained within it flew into his eyes before the wind could dissipate it. Amra, following her husband's directions, had collected a large amount from the fireplace's sand pile to wrap in it, and though it had made his head feel heavy it had been worth it.

Ezkr screamed and clutched at his eyes, releasing his dagger. At the same time, Green slid forward and rammed his fist into the man's groin. Then, as Ezkr crumpled toward him, he caught him and eased him down. He followed his first blow with a chopping of the edge of his palm against the fellow's neck. Ezkr quit screaming and passed out. Green rolled him over so that he lay on his stomach across the yard, supported on one side by the mast, with his legs, arms and head dangling. That was all he wanted to do for him. He had no intention of carrying him down. His only wish was to get to the deck, where he'd be safe. If Ezkr fell off now, too bad.

Amra and Inax were waiting at the foot of the shrouds when Green slowly climbed off. When he set foot on the deck, he thought his legs would give way, they were trembling so. Amra, noticing this, quickly put her arms around him as if to embrace the conquering hero but actually to help support him.

"Thanks," he muttered. "I need your strength, Amra."

"Anybody would who had done what you've done," she said. "But my strength and all of me is at your disposal, Alan."

The children were looking at him with wide, admiring eyes and yelling, "That's our daddy! Big blond Green! He's quick as a grass cat, bites like a dire dog and'll spit poison in your eye, like a flying snake!"

Then, in the next moment, he was submerged under the men and women of the Clan, all anxious to congratulate him for his feat and to call him brother. The only ones who did not crowd around, trying to kiss him on the lips, were the officers of the *Bird* and the wife and children of the unfortunate sailor, Ezkr. These were climbing up the rigging to fasten a rope around his waist and lower him.

There *was* one other who remained aloof. That was the harpist, Grazoot. He was still sulking at the foot of the mast.

Green decided that he'd better keep an eye on him, especially at night when a knife could be slipped between a sleeper's ribs and the body thrown overboard. He wished now that he'd not gone out of his way to insult the fellow's instrument, but at the time that had seemed the only thing to do. Now he had better try to find some way to pacify him.

13

TWO WEEKS of very hard work and little sleep passed as Green learned the duties of a topsailman. He hated to go aloft, but he found that being up so high had its advantages. It gave him a chance to catch a few winks now and then. There were many crow's nests where musketmen were stationed during a fight. Green would slip down into one of these and go to sleep at once. His foster son Grizquetr would stand watch for him, waking him if the foretop captain was coming through the rigging toward them. One afternoon Griz's whistle startled Green out of a sound sleep.

However, the captain stopped to give another sailor a lecture. Unable to go back to sleep, Green watched a herd of *hoobers* take to their hoofs at the approach of the *Bird*. These diminutive equines, beautiful with their orange bodies and black or white manes and fetlocks, sometimes formed immense herds that must have numbered in the hundreds of thousands. So thick were they that they looked like a bobbing sea of flashing heads and gleaming hoofs stretching clear to the horizon.

To stretch to the horizon was something on this planet. The plain was the flattest Green had ever seen. He could scarcely believe that it ran unbroken for thousands of miles. But it did, and from his high point of view he could see in a vast circle. It was a beautiful sight. The grass itself was tall and thickbodied, about two feet high and a sixteenth of an inch through. It was a bright green, brighter than earthly grass, almost shiny. During the rainy season, he was told, it would blossom with many tiny white and red flowers and give a pleasing perfume.

Now, as Green watched, something happened that startled him.

Abruptly, as if a monster mowing machine had come along the day before, the high grass ended and a lawn began. The new grass seemed to be only an inch high. And the lawn stretched at least a mile wide and as far ahead of the *Bird* as he could see.

"What do you think of that?" he asked Amra's son.

Grizquetr shrugged. "I don't know. The sailors say that it is done by the *wuru*, an animal the size of a ship, that only comes out at night. It eats grass, but it has the nasty temper of a dire dog, and will attack and smash a roller as if it were made of cardboard."

"Do you believe that?" Green said, watching him closely. Grizquetr was an intelligent lad in whom he hoped to plant a few seeds of skepticism. Perhaps some day those seeds might flower into the beginnings of science.

"I do not know if the story is true or not. It is possible, but I've met nobody who has ever seen a *wuru*. And if it comes out only at night, where does it hide during the daytime? There is no hole in the ground large enough to conceal it."

"Very good," said Green, smiling. Happily, Grizquetr smiled back. He worshiped his foster-father and nursed every bit of affection or compliment he got from him.

"Keep that open mind," said Green. "Neither believe nor disbelieve until you have solid evidence one way or another. And keep on remembering that new evidence may come up that will disprove the old and firmly established."

He smiled wryly. "I could use some of my own advice. I, for instance, had at one time absolutely refused to put any credence in what I have just seen with my own eyes. I put the story down as merely another idle story of those who sail the grassy seas. But I'm beginning to wonder if perhaps there couldn't be an animal of some kind like the *wuru*."

Both were silent for a while as they watched the animals race off like living orange rivers. Overhead, the birds wheeled in their hundreds of thousands of numbers. They, too, were beautiful, and even more colorful than the *hoobers*. Occasionally one lit in the rigging in a burst of dazzling feathers and a fury of melodious song or raucous screeches.

"Look!" said the boy, eagerly pointing. "A grass cat! He's been hiding, waiting to catch a *hoober,* and now he's afraid he'll be trampled to death by them."

Green's gaze followed the other's finger. He saw the long-legged, tiger-striped body loping desperately ahead of the thundering hoofs. It was completely closed in a pocket of the orange-maned beasts. Even as Green saw him, the sides of the pocket collapsed and the big cat disappeared from sight. If he remained alive he would do so through a miracle.

Suddenly, Grizquetr cried, "Gods!"

"What's the matter?" cried Green.

"On the horizon! A sail! It's shaped like a Ving sail!"

Others saw it too. The ship rang with shouts. A trumpeter blew battle stations; Miran's voice rose above those of others as he bellowed through a megaphone; chaos dissolved into order and purpose as everybody went to his appointed place. The animals, children and pregnant women were marshaled into the hold. The gun crews began unloading barrels of powder with a crane from a hatch. Musketmen swarmed up the rigging. The entire topmast crew tumbled aloft and took their places. As Green was already in his, he had some leisure to observe the whole outlay of preparations for fight. He watched Amra hurriedly give her children a kiss, make sure they'd all gone below, then begin tearing strips of cloth for bandages and of wadding for the muskets. Once she looked up and waved at him before turning back to her task. He waved back and got a severe reprimand from the top-captain for breaking discipline.

"An extra watch for you, Green, after this is over!"

The Earthman groaned and wished that the martinet would fall off and break every bone in his body. If he lost any more sleep . . . !

The day wore on as the strange ship came closer. Another sail appeared behind it, and the crew grew even tenser. From all appearances, they were being pursued by Vings. Vings usually went in pairs. Then there was the shape of the sails, which were narrower at bottom than at top. And there was the long, low streamlined hull and the overlarge wheels.

Nevertheless discipline was somewhat relaxed for a time. The pets and children were allowed to come up, and meals were prepared by the women. Even when the swifter craft came close enough so that the color of the sails was seen to be scarlet, there by confirming their suspicions of the strangers' identity, battle stations weren't recalled. Miran estimated that by the time the Vings were within cannon range night would fall.

"That is what they hate and what we love," he said, pacing back and forth, fingering his nose ring and blinking nervously his one good eye. "It'll be an hour before the big moon comes up. Not only that, it looks as though clouds may arise. See!" he cried to the first mate. "By Mennirox, is that not a wisp I detect in the northeast quarter?"

"By all the gods, I believe it is!" said the mate, peering upward, seeing nothing but clear sky, but hoping that wishing would make the clouds come true.

"Ah, Mennirox is good to his favorite worshiper!" said Miran. *"He that loves thee shall profit,* Book of the True Gods, Chapter Ten, Verse Eight. And Mennirox knows I love him with compound interest!"

"Yes, that he does," said the mate. "But what is your plan?"

"As soon as the last glow of the sun disappears completely from the horizon, so our silhouette won't be revealed, we'll swing and cut across their direct path of advance. We know that they'll be traveling fairly close together, hoping to catch up with us and blast us with crossfire. Well, we'll give them a chance, but we'll be gone before they can seize it. We'll go right between them in the dark and fire on both. By the time they're ready to reply in the dark we'll have slipped on by.

"And then," he whooped, slapping his fat thigh, "they'll probably cannonade each other to flinders, each thinking the other is us! Hoo, hoo, hoo!"

"Mennirox had better be with us," said the mate, paling. "It'll take damn tight calculating and more than a bit of luck. We'll be going by dead reckoning; not until we're almost on them will we see them; and if we're headed straight at them it'll be too late to avoid a collision. Wharoom! Smash! Boom! We're done for!"

"That's very true, but we're done for if we don't pull
some trick like that. They'll have caught us by dawn—they
can outmaneuver us—and they've more combined gunfire.
And though we'll fight like grass cats we'll go down, and
you know what'll happen then. The Vings don't take prisoners unless they're at the end of a cruise and going into
port."

"We should have accepted the Duke's offer of a convoy
of frigates," muttered the mate. "Even one would have been
enough to make the odds favor us."

"What? And lose half the profits of this voyage because
we have to pay that robber Duke for the use of his warships?
Have you lost your mind, mate?"

"If I have I'm not the only one," said the mate, turning
into the wind so his words were lost. But the helmsmen
heard him and reported the conversation later. In five minutes it was all over the ship.

"Sure, he's Greedyguts himself," the crew said. "But
then, we're his relatives; we know the value of a penny.
And isn't the fat old darling the daring one, though? Who
but a captain of the Clan Effenycan would think of such a
trick, and carry it through, too? And if he's such a money-
grabber, why, then, wouldn't he be afraid to risk his vessel
and cargo, not to mention his own precious blood, not to
mention the even more precious blood of his relatives? No,
Miran may be one-eyed and big-bellied and short of temper
and wind, but he's the man to hold down the foredeck.
Brother, dip me another glass from that barrel and let's toast
again the cool courage and hot avariciousness of Captain
Miran, Master Merchant."

Grazoot, the plump little harpist with the effeminate man-
ners, took his harp and began singing the song the Clan
loved most, the story of how they, a hill tribe, had come
down to the plains a generation ago. And how there they

had crept into the windbreak of the city of Chutlzaj and stolen a great windroller. And how they had ever since been men of the grassy seas, of the vast flat Xurdimur, and had sailed their stolen craft until it was destroyed in a great battle with a whole Krinkansprunger fleet. And how they had boarded a ship of the fleet and slain all the men and taken the women prisoners and sailed off with the ship right through the astounded fleet. And how they had taken the women as slaves and bred children and how the Effenycan blood was now half Krinkansprunger and that was where they got their blue eyes. And how the Clan now owned three big merchant ships—or had until two years ago when the other rolled over the green horizon during the Month of the Oak and were never heard of again, but they'd come back some day with strange tales and a hold brimming with jewels. And how the Clan now sailed under that mighty, grasping, shrewd, lucky, religious man, Miran.

Whatever else you could say about Grazoot, you could not deny that he had a fine baritone. Green, listening to his voice rise from the deck far below, could vision the rise and fall and rise again of these people and could appreciate why they were so arrogant and close-fisted and suspicious and brave. Indeed, if he had been born on this planet, he could have wanted no finer, more romantic, gypsyish life than that of a sailor on a windroller. Provided, that is, that he could get plenty of sleep.

The boom of a cannon disturbed his reverie. He looked up just in time to see the ball appear at the end of its arc and flash by him. It was not enough to scare him, but watching it plow into the ground about twenty feet away from the starboard steering wheel made him realize what damage one lucky shot could do.

However, the Ving did not try again. He was a canny pirate who knew better than to throw away ammunition. Doubtless he was hoping to panic the merchantman into a

frenzy of replies, powder-wasting and useless. Useless because the sun set just then and in a few minutes dusk was
gone and darkness was all around them. Miran didn't even
bother to tell his men to hold their fire, since they wouldn't
have dreamed of touching off the cannon until he gave the
word. Instead he repeated that no light should be shown
and that the children must go below decks and must be kept
quiet. No one was to make a noise.

Then, casting one last glance at the positions of the pur-
suing craft, now rapidly dissolving into the night, he estimated the direction and strength of the wind. It was as it
had been the day they set sail, an east wind dead astern, a
good wind, pushing them along at eighteen miles an hour.

Miran spoke in a soft voice to the first mate and the other
officers, and they disappeared into the darkness shrouding
the decks. They were giving prearranged orders, not by the
customary bellowing through a megaphone but by low voices
and touches. While they directed the crew, Miran stood
with bare feet upon the foredeck. He held a half-crouching
posture, and acted as if he were detecting the moves of the
invisible sailors by the vibrations of their activities running
through the wood of the decks and the spars and the masts
and up to his feet. Miran was a fat nerve center that gathered
in all the unspoken messages scattered everywhere through
the body of the *Bird*. He seemed to know exactly what he
was doing, and if he hesitated or doubted because of the
solid blackness around him, he gave the helmsmen no sign.
His voice was firm.

"Hold it steady."

"...six, seven, eight, nine, ten. Now! Swing her hard
aport! Hold her, hold her!"

To Green, high up on the topmost spar of the foremast,
the turning about seemed an awful and unnatural deed. He
could *feel* the hull, and with it his mast, of course, leaning

over and over, until his senses told him that they must inevitably capsize and send him crashing to the ground. But his senses lied, for though he seemed to fall forever, the time came when the journey back toward an upright position began. Then he was sure he would keep falling the other way, forever.

Suddenly the sails fluttered. The vessel had come into the dead spot where there was no wind acting upon her canvas. Then, as her original impetus kept her going, the canvas boomed, seeming to his straining and oversensitive ears like cannon firing. This time the wind was catching her from what was for her a completely unnatural direction, from dead ahead. As a result, the sails filled out backwards, and their middle portions pressed against the masts.

The 'roller came almost to a stop at once. The rigging groaned, and the masts themselves creaked loudly. Then they were bending backwards, while the sailors clinging to them in the darkness swore under their breaths and clamped down desperately on their handholds.

"Gods!" said Green. "What *is* he doing?"

"Quiet!" said a nearby man, the foretop-captain. "Miran is going to run her backwards."

Green gasped. But he made no further comment, trying to visualize what a strange sight the *Bird of Fortune* must be, and wishing it were daylight so he could see her. He sympathized with the helmsmen, who had to act against their entire training. It was a bad enough strain for them to try to sail blindly between two vessels. But to roll in reverse! They would have to put the helm to port when their reflexes cried out to them to put it to starboard, and vice versa! And no doubt Miran was aware of this and was warning them about it every few seconds.

Green began to see what was happening. By now the *Bird* was rolling on her former course, but at a reduced rate because the sails, bellying against their masts, would not offer as much surface to the wind. Therefore, the Ving vessels would by now be almost upon them, since the merchant ship had also lost much ground in her maneuver. In one or two minutes the Ving would overtake them, would for a short while ride side by side with them, then would pass.

Provided, of course, that Miran had estimated correctly his speed and rate of curve in turning. Otherwise they might even now expect a crash from the foredeck as the bow of the Ving caught them.

"Oh, Booxotr," prayed the foretop-captain. "Steer us right, else you lose your most devout worshiper, Miran."

Booxotr, Green recalled, was the God of Madness.

Suddenly a hand gripped Green's shoulder. It was the captain of the foretop.

"Don't you see them!" he said softly. "They're a blacker black than the night."

Green strained his eyes. Was it his imagination, or did he actually see something moving to his right? And another something, the hint of a hint, moving to his left?

Whatever it was, 'roller or illusion, Miran must have seen it also. His voice shattered the night into a thousand pieces, and it was never again the same.

"Cannoneers, fire!"

Suddenly it was as if fireflies had been in hiding and had swarmed out at his command. All along the rails little lights appeared. Green was startled, even though he knew that the punks had been concealed beneath baskets so that the Vings would have no warning at all.

Then the fireflies became long glowing worms, as the fuses took flame.

There was a great roar, and the ship rocked. Iron demons belched flame.

No sooner done than musketry broke out like a hot rash all over the ship. Green himself was part of this, blazing away at the vessel momentarily and dimly revealed by the light of the cannon fire.

Darkness fell, but silence was gone. The men cheered; the decks trembled as the big wooden trains holding the cannon were run back to the ports from which they'd recoiled. As for the pirates, there was no answering fire. Not at first. They must have been taken completely by surprise.

Miran shouted again; again the big guns roared.

Green, reloading his musket, found that he was bracing himself against a tendency to lean to the right. It was a few seconds before he could comprehend that the *Bird* was turning in that direction even though it was still going backwards.

"Why is he doing that?" he shouted.

"Fool, we can't roll up the sails, stop, then set sail again. We'd be right where we started, sailing backwards. We have to turn while we have momentum, and how better to do that than reverse our maneuver? We'll swing around until we're headed in our original direction."

Green understood now. The Vings had passed them, therefore they were in no danger of collision with them. And they couldn't continue sailing backwards all night. The thing to do now would be to cut off at an angle so that at daybreak they'd be far from the pirates.

At that moment cannonfire broke out to their left. The men aboard the *Bird* refrained from cheering only because of Miran's threats to maroon them on the plain if they did anything to reveal their position. Nevertheless they all bared their teeth in silent laughter. Crafty old Miran had sprung his best trap. As he'd hoped, the two pirates, unaware that their attacker was now behind them, were shooting each other.

"Let them bang away until they blow each other sky-high," chortled the foretop-master. "Ah, Miran, what a tale we'll have to tell in the taverns when we get to port."

14

FOR FIVE MINUTES the intermittent flashes and bellows told that the Vings were still hammering away. Then the dark took hold again. Apparently the two had either recognized each other or else had decided that night fighting was a bad business and had steered away from each other. If this last was true, then they wouldn't be much to fear, for one Ving wouldn't attack the merchant by itself.

The clouds broke, and the big and the little moons spread brightness everywhere. The pirate vessels were not in sight. Nor were they seen when dawn broke. There was sail half a mile away, but this alarmed no one, except the untutored Green, because they recognized its shape as a sister. It was a merchant from the nearby city of Dem, of the Dukedom of Potzihili.

Green was glad. They could sail with it. Safety in numbers.

But no. Miran, after hailing it and finding that it also was going to Estorya, ordered every bit of canvas crowded on in an effort to race away from it.

"Is he crazy?" groaned Green to a sailor.

"Like a *zilmar*," replied the sailor, referring to a foxlike animal that dwelt in the hills. "We must get to Estorya first if we would realize the full value of our cargo."

"Utter featherbrained folly," snarled Green. "That ship doesn't carry live fish. It can't possibly compete with us."

"No, but we've other things to sell. Besides, it's in Miran's blood. If he saw another merchant pass him he'd come down sick."

Green threw his hands into the air and rolled his eyes in despair. Then he went back to work. There was much to do yet before he'd be allowed to sleep.

The days and nights passed in the hard routine of his labor and the alarms and excursions that occasionally broke up the routine. Now and then the gig was launched, while the 'roller was in full speed, and it sped away under the power of its white fore-and-aft sail. It would be loaded with hunters, who would chase a *hoober* or deer or pygmy hog until it became exhausted; then would shoot the tired animal. They always brought back plenty of fresh meat. As for water, the catchtanks on the decks were full because it rained at least half an hour at every noon and dusk.

Green wondered at the regularity and promptness of these showers. The clouds would appear at twelve, it would rain for thirty to sixty minutes, then the sky would clear again. It was all very nice, but it was also very puzzling.

Sometimes he was allowed to try target practice from the crow's nest on the grass cats or the huge dire dogs. These latter ran in packs of half a dozen to twenty, and would often pace the *Bird*, howling and growling and sometimes running between the wheels. The sailors had quite a few tales of what they did to people who fell overboard or were wrecked on the plains.

Green shuddered and went back to his target practice. Though he ordinarily was against shooting animals just for the fun of it, he had no compunction about putting a ball through these wolfish-looking creatures. Ever since he'd been tormented by Alzo he'd hated dogs with a passion unbecoming to a civilized man. Of course, the fact that every canine on the planet instinctively loathed him because of his Earthman odor and did his best to sink his teeth into him, strengthened Green's reaction. His legs were always healing from bites of the pets aboard.

Often the 'roller would cruise through grass tall as a man's knee. Then suddenly it would pass onto one of those tremendous lawns which seemed so well kept. Green had never ceased puzzling about them, but all he could get from anyone was one or more variations of the fable of the *wuru*, the herbivore bigger than two ships put together.

One day they passed a wreck. Its burned hulk lay sideways on the ground, and here and there bones gleamed in the sun. Green expressed surprise that the masts, wheels and cannon were gone. He was told that those had been taken away by the savages who roamed the plains.

"They use the wheels for their own craft, which are really nothing but large sailing platforms, land-rafts, you might say," Amra told him. "On these they pitch their tents and their fireplaces, and from them they go forth to hunt. Some of them, however, disdain platforms and make their homes upon the 'roaming islands.'"

Green smiled but said nothing about that fairy story because disbelief excited these people, even Amra.

"You'll not see many wrecks," she continued. "Not because there aren't many, for there are. Out of every ten 'rollers that leave for distant breaks, you can expect only six to get back."

"That few? I'm amazed that with such a casualty ratio you could get anybody to risk his fortune and life."

"You forget that he who comes back is many times richer than when he sailed away. Look at Miran. He is taxed heavily at every port of call. He is taxed even more heavily in his home port. And he has to split with the Clansmen, though he does get a tenth of the profit of every cargo. Despite this, he is the richest man in Quotz, richer even than the Duke."

"Yes, but a man is a fool to take risks like these just for the remote chance of a fortune," he protested. Then he stopped. After all, for what other reason had the Norsemen gone to America, and Columbus to the West Indies? Or why were so many hundreds of thousands of Earthmen daring the perils of interstellar space? What about himself, for instance? He'd left a stable and well-paying job on Earth as a specialist in raising sea crops to go to Pushover, a planet of Albireo. He'd expected to make his fortune there after two years of not-too-hard work and then retire. If only that accident hadn't happened . . . !

Of course, some of the pioneers weren't driven by the profit motive. There was such a thing as love of adventure. Not a pure love, however. Even the most adventurous saw Eldorado gleaming somewhere in the wilds. Greed conquered more frontiers than curiosity.

"You'd think the ruins of 'rollers would not be rare, even if these plains are vast," said Amra, breaking in on his reflections. "But the savages and pirates must salvage them as fast as they're made."

"Your pardon, Mother, for interrupting," said Grizquetr. "I heard a sailor, Zoob, remark on that very thing just the other day. he said that he once saw a 'roller that had been gutted, by pirates, he supposed. It was three days' journey out of Yeshkayavach, the city of quartz in the far North. He said their 'roller was a week there, then returned on the same route. But when they came to where the wreck had been it was gone, every bit of it. Even the bones of the dead sailors were missing."

"And he said that that reminded him of a story his father had told him when he was young. He said his father told him that his ship had once almost run into a huge uncharted hole in the plain. It was big, at least two hundred feet across, and earth had been piled up outside, like the crater of a volcano. At first that was what they thought it was, a volcano just beginning, even though they'd never heard of such a thing on the Xurdimur. Then they met a ship whose men had seen the hole made. It was caused, they said by a mighty falling star..."

"A meteor," commented Green.

"...and it had dug that great hole. Well, that was as good an explanation as any. But the amazing thing was that when they came by that very spot a month later, the hole was gone. It was filled up and smoothed out, and grass was growing over it as if nothing had ever broken the skin of the earth. Now, how do you explain that, Foster-father?"

"There are more things in heaven and earth than ever your philosophies dreamed of, Horatio," Green nonchalantly replied, though he felt as though he wasn't quoting exactly right.

Amra and her son blinked. "Horatio?"

"Never mind."

"This sailor said that it was probably the work of the gods, who labor secretly at night that the plain may stay flat and clean of obstacles so their true worshipers may sail upon it and profit thereby."

"Will the wonders of rationalization never cease?" said Green.

He rose from his pile of furs. "Almost time for my watch." He kissed Amra, the maid, the children, and stepped out from the tent. He walked rather carelessly across the deck absorbed in wondering what the effect would be upon Amra if he told her his true origin. Could she comprehend the concept of other worlds existing by the hundreds of thousands, yet so distant from each other that a man could walk steadily for a million years and still not get halfway from Earth to this planet of hers? Or would she react automatically, as most of her fellows would do, and think that he must surely be a demon in human disguise? It would be more natural for her to prefer the latter idea. If you looked at it objectively, it *was* more plausible, given her lack of scientific knowledge. Much more believable, too.

Somebody bumped him. Jarred out of his reverie, he automatically apologized in English.

"Don't curse at me in your foreign tongue!" snarled Grazoot, the plump little harpist.

Ezkr was standing behind Grazoot. He spoke out of the side of his mouth, urging the bard on. "He thinks he can walk all over you, Grazoot, because he insulted your harp once and you let him get away with it."

Grazoot puffed out his cheeks, reddened in the face and glared. "It is only because Miran has forbidden duels that I have not plunged my dagger into this son of an *izzot!*"

Green looked from one to the other. Obviously this scene was prearranged with no good end for him in view.

"Stand aside," he said haughtily. "You are interfering with the discipline of the 'roller. Miran will not like that."

"Indeed!" said Grazoot. "Do you think Miran cares at all about what happens to you? You're a lousy sailor and it hurts me to have to call you brother. In fact, I spit every time I say it to you, brother!"

Grazoot did just that. Green, who was downwind, felt the fine mist wet his legs. He began to get angry.

"Out of my way or I'll report you to the first mate," he said firmly and walked by them. They gave way, but he had an uneasy feeling in the small of his back, as if a knife would plunge into it. Of course, they shouldn't be so foolish, because they would be hamstrung and then dropped off the 'roller for the crime of cowardice. But these people were so hotheaded they were just as likely as not to stab him in a moment of fury.

Once on the rope ladder that ran up to the crow's nest, he began to lose the prickly feeling in his back. At that moment Grazoot called out, "Oh, Green, I had a vision last night, a true vision, because my patron god sent it, and he himself appeared in it. He announced that he would snuff up his nostrils the welcome scent of your blood, spilled all over the deck from your fall!"

Green paused with one foot on the rail. "You tell your god to stay away from me, or I'll punch him in the nose!" he called back.

There was a gasp from the many people who'd gathered around to listen. "Sacrilege!" yelled Grazoot. "Blasphemy!" He turned to those around him. "Did you hear that?"

"Yes," said Ezkr, stepping out from the crowd. "I heard him and I am shocked. Men have burned for less."

"Oh, my patron god, Tonuscala, punish this pride-swollen man! Make your dreams come true. Cast him headlong from the mast and dash him to the deck and break every bone in his body so that men may learn that one does not mock the true gods."

"Tahkhai," murmured the crowd. "Amen."

Green smiled grimly. He had fallen into their trap and now must be on guard. Plainly, one or both of them would be aloft tonight during the dark hour after sunset, and they'd be content with nothing less than pitching him out over the deck. His death would be considered to have come from the hands of an outraged god. And if Amra should accuse

Ezkr and Grazoot she'd get little justice. As for Miran, the fellow would probably heave a sigh of relief, because he'd be rid of a troublesome fellow who could carry damaging stories of a certain conspiracy to the Duke of Tropat.

He climbed up to the crow's nest, and settled gloomily to staring off at the horizon. Just before sunset Grizquetr came up with a bottle of wine and food in a covered basket.

Between bites Green told the boy of his suspicions.

"Mother has already guessed as much," said the lad. "She is a very clever woman indeed, my mother. She has put a curse upon the two if you should come to harm."

"Very clever. That will do a great deal of good. Thank her for her splendid work while you're picking up my pieces from the deck, will you?"

"To be sure," replied Grizquetr, trying hard to keep his sober face from breaking into a grin. "And Mother also sent you this."

He rolled the kerchief all the way off the top of the basket. Green's eyes widened.

15

"A ROCKET FLARE!"

"Yes. Mother says that you are to release it when you hear the bos'n's whistle from the deck."

"Now, why in the world would I do that? Won't I get into tremendous trouble by doing that? I'll be run through the gauntlet a dozen times for that. No sir, not me. I've seen those poor fellows after the whips were through with them."

"Mother said for me to tell you that nobody will be able to prove who sent up the flare."

"Perhaps. It sounds reasonable. But why should I do it?"

"It will light up the whole ship for a minute, and everybody will be able to see that Ezkr and Grazoot are in the rigging. The whole ship will be in an uproar. Of course, when it is discovered that somebody has stolen two flares from the storeroom, and when a search is conducted, and one flare is found hidden in Ezkr's trunk, then . . . well, you see . . ."

"Oh, beamish boy!" chortled Green. "Calloo, callay! Go tell your mother she's the most marvelous woman on this planet—though that's really not much of a compliment, now I think of it. Oh, wait a minute! About this bos'n's whistle. Now, why should he be warning me to send up a flare?"

"He won't. Mother will be blowing it. She'll be waiting for a signal from me or Azaxu," Grizquetr said, referring to his younger brother. "We'll be watching Ezkr and Grazoot, and when they start to climb aloft we'll notify her. She'll wait until she thinks they're about halfway up, then she'll whistle."

"That woman has saved my life at least half a dozen times. What would I do without her?"

"That's what Mother said. She said that she doesn't know why she went after you when you tried to run away from her—from us—because she has great pride. And she doesn't have to chase a man to get one; princes have begged her to come live with them. But she did because she loves you, and a good thing, too. Otherwise your stupidity would have killed you ten times over by now."

"Oh, she did, did she? Well, hah, hum. Yes, well . . . !"

Thoroughly ashamed of himself, yet angry at Amra for her estimate of him, Green miserably watched Grizquetr climb down the ratlines.

During the next half-hour, time seemed to coagulate, to thicken and harden around him so that he felt as if he were encased in it. The clouds that always came up after sunset formed, and a light drizzle began. It would last for about an hour, he knew, then the clouds would disappear so swiftly that they would give the impression of being yanked away like a tablecloth by some magician over the horizon. But he'd cram a highly nervous lifetime into those minutes, wondering if perhaps there wouldn't be some unforeseen frustration of Amra's schedule.

The first webby drops struck his face, and he wondered if perhaps that wouldn't be what the two would wait for. They'd probably taken the first step up the rigging, but he mustn't expect her whistle for some time yet. If they were clever they wouldn't climb up directly beneath him, but would go aft, ascend to the top, then climb over to him. It was true that they'd have to pass others who, like Green, were also stationed aloft on watch. But Ezkr and Grazoot knew the locations of these. So dark was it they could pass within touching distance and not be seen or heard. The wind in the rigging, the creak of masts, the rumble of the great wheels would drown out any slight noise they might make.

The 'roller did not stop sailing just because the helmsmen could not see. The *Bird* followed a well-charted route; every permanent obstacle along here had been memorized by helmsmen and officers alike. If anything formidable was expected in their path during the dark period, a course would be set to avoid it. The officers on duty would advise the helmsmen on their steering by means of an ingenious dial on a notched plate. His sensitive fingers, following its flickerings back and forth, and comparing them with the directional notches, would tell him how close to the course they were keeping. The dial itself was fixed to the needle of a compass beneath it.

Green hunched his shoulders beneath his coat and walked around the walls of his nest. He strained his eyes to make out something in the blackness that wrapped him around like a shroud. There was nothing, nothing at all. . . . No, wait! What was that? A vague outline of a white face?

He stared hard until it disappeared, then he sighed and realized how rigidly he'd been standing there. And of course he'd been open to attack from behind all that time.

No, not really. If he couldn't see an arm's length away, neither could the other two.

But they didn't have to see. They knew the ropes so well that they could grope blindfolded to his nest and there feel him out. A touch of a finger, followed by a thrust of steel. That would be all it would take.

He was thinking of that when he felt the finger. It poked into his back and held him like a statue for just a second, quivering, paralyzed. Then he gave a hoarse cry and jumped away. He snatched out his dagger and crouched down close to the floor, straining his eyes and ears, trying to detect them. Surely, if they were breathing as hard as he, he couldn't fail to hear them.

On the other hand, he realized with a sudden sickishness, they could hear him just as well.

"Come on! Come on!" he said soundlessly, through clenched teeth. "Do something! Make a move so I can pin you, you sons of *izzots!*"

Perhaps they were doing the same, waiting for him to betray himself. The best thing was to hug the floor where he was and hope they'd stumble over him.

He kept reaching out in front of him, feeling for the warm flesh of a face. His other hand held his dagger.

It was during one of his tentative explorations that he felt the basket where Grizquetr had left it. At once, seized with what he thought was an inspiration, he pulled out the flare. Why wait for them to close in on him and butcher him like a hog? He'd send up the flare now, and in the first shock of its glare he'd attack them.

The only trouble was, he'd have to put down his dagger in order to take his flint and steel and tinderbox from his pocket. He hated not to have it ready for thrusting.

Solving this problem by putting the dagger between his teeth, he took out his firebox, paused, and swiftly put them back. Now, how was he supposed to get the tinder going when it was drizzling? That was one thing Amra, with all her cleverness, hadn't thought of.

"Fool!" he whispered to himself. "I'm the fool!" And in the next moment, he was removing his coat and putting the flint and steel and box under its protecting cover. He couldn't see what he was doing, but if he held the tinder close enough a spark should fall on it. Then he'd have a flame hot enough to touch off the fuse of the flare.

Again, he froze. His enemies were waiting for him to reveal himself through noise. What better giveaway than flint scraping against steel? And what about the sound of the rocket flare's spiked support being driven into the wooden floor?

He suppressed a groan. No matter what he did he was leaving himself wide open.

It was then that the shrillness of a whistle below startled him. He rose, wondering frenziedly what he should do next. So convinced was he that Ezkr and Grazoot were poised just outside the nest, he could not believe that Amra had not misjudged the time it had taken them to climb to him or that she had not been held up for some reason and now was frantically trying to warn him.

But, he realized, he couldn't just stand there like a scared sheep. Whether Amra was right or not, whether they were within dagger's thrust or not, he had to take action.

"Do your damndest!" he growled at whatever might be in the dark, and he struck steel against flint. The materials were under his coat, blocking his view, but he lay down again so he could see between his arms and under the coat held over them. The tinder caught at once and blazed up, then began a small but steady glow in the harder wood of the box. Without waiting to look around, Green rammed the flare's spike into the deck of the nest. Swiftly he brought the punk up, still holding the coat over it for protection from the drizzle and also from any watching eyes. He held it against the fuse, saw the cord catch flame and sizzle like a frying worm. Then he had ducked around the other side of the mast that supported the nest, for he knew how unpredictable these primitive rockets were. Like as not it would go off in his face. Hardly had he rounded the big pillar of the mast when he heard a soft whooshing sound. He looked up just in time to see the rocket explode in a white glare. The moment it dispelled the darkness he jerked his head to the right and the left in an effort to see if Ezkr and Grazoot were on him, as he'd *known* they must be.

But they weren't. They were still half a ship's length away from him, caught by the light in the rigging, like flies in a spider's web. What he had thought was a finger poking him in the back must have been the bolt that held the support for the muskets which were to be fired from the nest during combat.

So relieved was he, he would have broken into loud laughter, but at that moment a great cry broke from the decks below. The mate and the helmsmen were shouting in alarm.

16

THEN THE FLARE had died and had left nothing but its after-image on the eye—and panic on the brain.

Green did not know what to make of it. In the first instant he had thought that it was the 'roller alone that was speeding toward an uncharted forest-grown hill. Immediately after, he'd seen that his senses were deceiving him and that the mass was also moving. It had looked like a hill, or several hills, sliding across the grass toward them. But even as the darkness came back he'd seen that there were other hills behind it, and that the whole thing was actually a sort of iceberg of rocks and of soil from which grew trees.

That was all he could make out in that confusing moment. Even then he couldn't believe it, because a mountain just didn't run along of its own volition on flat land.

Credible or not, it was not being ignored by the helmsmen. They must have turned the wheel almost at once, for Green could feel the leaning of the mast to port and the shift of wind upon his face. The *Bird* was swinging to the southwest in an effort to avoid the "roaming island." Unfortunately it was too dark for the men to have worked swiftly in trimming the sails even if a full crew had been aloft. And there were far too few on the top, as it was not thought necessary to have them on duty when the 'roller was running in the post-sunset drizzle.

Green had time for one short prayer—no nonsense about punching a god in the nose, now—and then he was hurled against the wall of the nest. There was the loudest noise he'd ever heard—the loudest because it was the crack of doom for him. Rope split like a giant's whip cracking; spars, suddenly released from the rigging, strummed like monster violins; the masts, falling down, thundered; intermingled with all that were the screams of the people below on the deck and in the holds. Green himself was screaming as he felt the foremast lean over, and he slid from the floor of the nest, which had suddenly threatened to become a wall, and fought to hold himself on the wall, which had now become a floor. His fingers closed upon the musket-support with the desperation of one who clings to the only solid thing in the world.

For a minute, the mast stopped its forward movement, held taut by the tangled mass of ropes. Green hoped that he was safe, that all the damage had been done.

But no, even as he dared think he might come out alive, the mighty grinding noise began again. The island of rock and trees was continuing its course and was smashing the hull of the ship beneath it, gobbling up wheels, axles, keel, timber, cargo, cannon and people.

The next he knew, he was flying through the air, torn from his hold, catapulted far away from the 'roller. It seemed as if he actually soared, gained altitude, though this must have been an illusion. Then the hard return to earth, the impact on his face, his body, his legs. The outstretched arms to soften the blow that must surely splinter his bones and pulp his flesh. The pitiful arms, the last warding-off gesture before annihilation. The series of hard blows, like many fists. The sudden realization that he was among tree branches and that his fall was being broken by them. His trying to grab one to hang on and its slipping away and his continued rapid and punishing descent.

Then, oblivion.

He didn't know how long he'd been unconscious, but when he sat up he saw through the trunks of the trees the shattered hull of the *Bird* about a hundred feet away. It was lying on its side on a lower level than he was, so he supposed that he was sitting on the slope of a hill. Only half of the craft was in sight; it must have been broken in two, and most of the middeck and stern ground into rubble beneath the advancing juggernaut of the island.

Dully, he realized that the drizzle had stopped, the clouds had cleared and the big and little moons were up. The seeing was good, too good.

There were people left alive in the wreck, men, women and children who were trying to climb through the tangle of ropes, spars and broken, jagged, projecting planks. Screams, moans, shouts and calls for help made a chaos.

Groaning, he managed to rise to his feet. He had a very painful headache. One eye was so swollen he couldn't see with it. He tasted blood in his mouth and felt several broken teeth with his lacerated tongue. His sides hurt when he breathed. The skin seemed to have been torn off the palms of his hands. His right knee must have been wrenched, and his left heel was a ball of fire. Nevertheless he got up. Amra and Paxi and her other children were in there; that is, unless they'd been caught in the other half. He had to find out. Even if they were beyond his help there were others who weren't.

He started to hobble through the trees. Then he saw a man step out from behind a bush. Thinking that he must be a survivor who had wandered off in a dazed condition, Green opened his mouth to speak to him. But there was something odd about him that imposed silence. He looked closer. Yes, the fellow wore a headdress of feathers and held a long spear in his hand. And the moonlight, where it slipped through the branches and shone upon an exposed shoulder, gleamed red, white, blue-black, yellow and green. The man was painted all over with stripes of different colors!

Green slowly sank down upon his hands and knees behind a bush. It was then that he became aware of others who stood behind trees and watched the wreck. Then these emerged from the darkness under the branches. Presently, at least fifty plumed, painted, armed men were gathered together, all silent, all intently inspecting the wreck and the survivors.

One raised a spear as a signal and gave a loud, whooping war cry. The others echoed him, and when he ran out from beneath the branches they followed him.

Green could watch only for a minute before he had to close his eyes.

"No, no!" he moaned. "The children, too!"

When he forced himself to look again, he saw that he had been mistaken in thinking that everybody had been put to spear. After the first vicious onslaught, in which they'd killed indiscriminately and hysterically, like all undisciplined primitives, they'd spared the younger women and the little girls. Those able to walk were lined up and marched off under the guard of half a dozen spearsmen. The too badly injured were run through on the spot.

Even in the midst of this scene, Green felt some of his

intense anguish eased a little. Amra was still alive!

She held Paxi in one arm and with the other pulled Soon, her daughter by the temple sculptor. Though she must have been terribly frightened, she faced her captors with the same proud bearing she'd always had, whether in the presence of peasant or prince. Inzax, her maid, stood behind her.

Green decided that he'd better try to follow her and her captors at a discreet distance. But before he could get away he saw the women and older children of the savages appear, bearing torches. Fortunately none came his way. Some of these mutilated the dead, dancing around the hacked corpses and howling in imitation of the adult men. Then began the work in earnest, the carving up of the flesh. These painted people were cannibals and made no bones about it. Fires were being lit for a midnight snack before the bulk of the meat was brought back to wherever their homes were.

17

GREEN STAYED FAR enough behind the prisoners and savages to keep out of sight if any man should turn. The path was narrow, winding between crowding trunks and under low branches. The soil underfoot was rich and springy, as if composed of generations of leaves. Green estimated he must have gone at least a mile and a half, not as the crow flies, but more like a drunk trying to find his way home. Then, without warning, the forest stopped and a clearing was before him. In the midst of this stood a village of about ten log houses with thatched roofs. Six were rather small outhouses serving one purpose or another. The four large ones were, he guessed, long houses for community living. They were grouped about a central spot in which were the remains of several large fires beneath big iron pots and spits. Clay tanks were scattered here and there; these held rain water. Before each house was a twenty-foot-high totem pole, brightly painted, and around it many slender poles holding skulls.

The prisoners were led into one of the outhouses and the door barred. A man stationed himself at the front, squatting with his back to the wall and holding a spear in one hand. The others greeted the old women and younger children who had been left behind. Though they spoke in a language Green didn't understand, they were obviously describing what they'd found at the wreck. Some of the old crones then began piling brushwood and small logs under one of the huge iron kettles; presently they had a fire blazing brightly. Others brought out glasses and cups of precious metals—loot from wrecks. These they filled with some sort of liquor, probably a native beer, judging from the foam that spilled over the sides. One of the young boys began idly tapping upon a drum and soon was beating out a monotonous simple rhythm. It looked as if they were going to make a night of it.

But after a few drinks the warriors arose, picked up jugs of liquor and walked into the woods, leaving one man to guard the prisoners' hut. All the children over the age of four left with them, trailing along in the dark, though the warriors made no effort to slow their pace so the children could keep up.

Green waited until he was sure the spearsmen were some distance away, then rose. His muscles protested at any movement, and pains shot through his head, knee and ankle. But he ignored them and limped around the edge of the clearing until he came to the back of one of the long houses.

He slipped inside and stood by the side of the doorway. It was more illuminated than he'd thought at first, because of the several large and open windows which admitted moonbeams. Hens sleepily clucked at him, and one of the midget pigs grunted questioningly. Suddenly something soft brushed across his ankles. Startled, he jumped to one side. His heart, which had been beating fast enough before, threatened to hammer a hole in his ribs. He crouched, straining to see what it was. Then a soft meowing nearby told him. He relaxed a little and stretched out a hand, saying, "Here, kitty, kitty, come here."

But the cat walked by, his tail raised and a look of disdain on his face as he disappeared through the door. Seeing the animal reminded Green of something about which he was anxious. That was whether the natives kept dogs or not. He hadn't seen any and thought that surely if there were some he'd have long ago heard the noisy beasts. Undoubtedly, by now, he should have a whole pack of the obnoxious monsters snarling at his heels.

Silently, he walked into the long single room with its high ceiling. From thick rafters hung rolled-up curtains, which he supposed would be let down to make a semi-private room for any families that wished it. From them also hung vegetables, fruit and meat; chickens, rabbits, piglets, squirrels, *hoober* and venison. There were no human parts, so he guessed that the flesh of man was not so much a staple diet to these people as a food for religious purposes.

All he did know was that he would have to take some meat with him. He gathered strips of dried *hoober,* rolled them into a ball and stuffed them in a bag. Then he took down an iron-headed spear and a sharp steel knife from their rack on the wall. Knife in belt and spear in hand, he went out the back door.

Outside, he stopped to listen to the far-off beating of drums and the chanting of voices. There must be quite a celebration around the wreck.

"Good," he muttered to himself. "If they get drunk and pass out I'll have time for what I want to do."

Staying well within the shadows of the trees, he picked his way to the back of the hut in which the prisoners were.

From where he stood he could see that there were only six old women—about all the island's economy could afford, he supposed—and some ten infants, all toddlers. Most of these, once the excitement caused by the noisy warriors had subsided with their leavetaking, had lain down close to the fire and gone to sleep. The only one who might give real trouble, aside from the guard, was a boy of ten, the one who was now tapping softly on the drum. At first Green could not understand why he hadn't gone with the others of his age to the wreck. But the empty stare and the unblinking way he looked into the fire showed why. Green had no doubt that if he were to come close enough to the lad, he'd see that the eyeballs were filmed over with white. Blindness was nothing rare on this filthy planet.

Satisfied as to everybody's location, he crept to the back of the hut and examined the walls. They were made of thick poles driven into the ground and bound together with rope taken from a 'roller's rigging. There were plenty of openings for him to look through, but it was so dark that he could see only the vague outlines moving about.

He put his mouth to one of the holes and said softly, "Amra!"

Somebody gasped. A little girl began to cry but was quickly hushed up. Amra answered, faint with joy.

"Alan! It can't be *you!*"

"I am not thy father's ghost!" he replied, and wondered at the same time how he could manage to inject any levity at all into the midst of this desperate situation. He was always doing it. Perhaps it was not the product of a true humor but more like the giggle of a person who was embarrassed or under some other stress, more the result of hysteria than anything else, his particular type of safety valve.

"Here's what I'm going to do," he said. "Listen carefully, then repeat it after me so I'll know you have it down."

She had to hear it only once to give it back to him letter-perfect. He nodded. "Good girl. I'm going now."

"Alan!"

"Yes?" he replied impatiently.

"If this doesn't work... if anything should happen to you... or me... remember that I love you."

He sighed. Even in the midst of this the eternal feminine emerged.

"I love you, too. But that hasn't got much to do with this situation."

Before she could answer and waste more valuable time he slid away, crawling on all fours around the corner of the hut. When he was where one more pace would have brought him into view of the guard and the old crones, he stopped. All this while he'd been counting the seconds. As soon as he'd clocked five minutes—which he thought would never pass—he rose and stepped swiftly around the corner, spear held in front of him.

The guard was drinking out of his mug with his eyes closed and his throat exposed. He fell over with Green's spear plunged through his windpipe, just above the breast-bone. The mug fell onto his lap and gushed its amber and foam over his legs.

Green withdrew the blade and whirled, ready to run upon anybody who started to flee. But the old women were huddled on their knees around a large board on which they were rolling some flour, cackling and talking shrilly. The blind boy continued tapping, his open eyes glaring into the fire. Only one saw Green, a boy of about three. Thumb in mouth, he stared with great round eyes at this stranger. But he was either too horrified to utter a sound or else he did not understand what had happened and was waiting to find out his elders' reactions before he offered his own.

Green lifted one finger to his lips in the universal sign of silence, then turned and lifted up the bar over the door.

Amra rushed out and took the guard's spear from her husband. The dead man's knife went to Inzax and his other knife to Aga, a tall, muscular woman who was captain of the female deck hands and who had once killed a sailor while defending her somewhat dubious honor.

At the same time, the chattering of the hags stopped. Green whirled around, and the silence was broken by shrieks. Frantically, the hags tried to scramble up from their stiffened knees and run away. But Green and the women were upon them before they could take more than a few steps. Not one of them reached the forest. It was grim work, one in which the Effenycan woman took fierce joy.

Without wasting a look on the poor old carcasses, Green rounded up the children and the blind boy and put them in the prisoners' hut. He had to hold Aga back from slaughtering them. Amra, he was pleased to see, had made no motion to help them in their intended butchery. She, understanding his brief look, replied, "I could not kill a child, even the spawn of these fiends. It would be like stabbing Paxi."

Green saw one of the women holding his daughter. He ran to her, took Paxi out of her arms and kissed the baby. Soon, Amra's ten-year-old child by the sculptor came shyly and stood by his side, waiting to be noticed. He kissed her, too. "You're getting to be a big girl, Soon," he said. "Do you suppose you could tag along behind your mother and carry Paxi for her? She has to carry her spear."

The girl, a big-eyed, redheaded beauty, nodded and took the baby.

Green eyed the long houses with the idea of setting them afire. He decided not to when it became apparent that the wind would carry sparks to the hut in which the savages' children were. Moreover, though a fire would undoubtedly create consternation among the roisterers at the wreck and keep them busy for some time, it would also cause them to start tracking down the refugees just that much sooner. Besides, there was the possibility of setting fire to the forest, wet though it was. He didn't want to destroy his only hiding-place.

He directed some women to go into the long house and load themselves with as much food and weapons as they could carry. In a few minutes he had the party ready to leave.

"We'll take this path that leads out of the village away from the path that goes to the wreck," he said. "Let's hope it goes to the other edge of the island, where we may find some small 'rollers on which we can escape. I presume these savages have some kind of sailing craft."

This path was as narrow and winding as the other one. It worked in the general direction of the western shore, and the savages were on the eastern shore.

Their way at first led upward, sometimes through passes formed by two large rocks. Several times they had to skirt little lakes, catch basins for rain. Once a fish flopped out of the water, scaring them. The island was fairly self-sufficient, what with its fish, rabbits, squirrels, wild fowl, pigs and various vegetables and fruit. He estimated that if the village was in the center of the island, then the mass should have a surface area of about one and a half square miles. Rough though the land was and thickly covered with grass, the place should offer cover for one refugee.

For one, yes, but not for six women and eight children.

18

AFTER MUCH PUFFING and panting, muttered encouragements to each other, and occasional cursing, they finally reached the summit of the tallest hill. Abruptly, they found themselves facing a clearing which ran around its crown. Directly ahead of them was a forest of totem poles, all gleaming palely in the moonlight. Beyond it was the dark yawning of a large cave.

Green walked out from the shadows of the branches to take a closer look. When he came back he said, "There's a little hut by the side of the cave. I looked in the window. An old woman's asleep in it. But her cats are wide-awake and likely to wake her up."

"All those totem poles bear the heads of cats," said Aga. "This place must be their holy of holies. It's probably taboo to all but the old priestess."

"Maybe so," replied Green. "But they must hold religious services of some sort here. There's a big pile of human skulls on the other side of the cave mouth, and also a stake covered with bloodstains.

"We can do two things. Go on down the other side of this hill, jump off onto the plain and take our chances there. Or else hide inside the cave and hope that because it's taboo nobody will explore it to look for us."

"It seems to me that's the first place they'd look into," said Aga.

"Not if we don't wake the old woman. Then if the savages come along later and ask her if anybody's come by they'll get no for an answer."

"What about the cats?"

Green shrugged his shoulders. "We'll have to take that chance. Perhaps, if once we get by them and into the cave, they may quiet down."

He was referring to their caterwauling, which was beginning to sound dreadful.

"No," said Aga, "that noise will be a signal to the islanders. They'll know something's up."

"Well," replied Green, "I don't know what you intend doing, but I'm going into that cave. I'm too tired to run any further."

"So are we," affirmed the other women. "We've reached the end of our strength."

There was a silence, and into that silence came a voice, a man's.

It whispered, "Please do not be startled. Be quiet. It is I. . . ."

Miran stepped out of the shadows behind them, holding his finger to his lips, his one eye round and pale in the moonlight. He was a ragged captain, not at all the elegantly uniformed commander of the *Bird of Fortune* and the wealthy-appearing patriarch of the Clan Effenycan. But he carried in his other hand a canvas bag. Green, seeing it, knew that Miran had managed somehow not only to escape with his skin but had also carried off a treasure in jewels.

"Behold," he announced, waving the bag, "all is not lost."

Green thought that he was referring to the jewels. However, Miran had turned and beckoned to someone in the darkness behind him.

Out of it slipped Grizquetr. Tears shone in his eyes as he ran to his mother and fell into her arms.

Amra began weeping softly. Until now she had repressed her grief over the children she thought forever lost to her. All thought had been directed to saving her own life and the lives of the two girls who had survived with her. Now, seeing her eldest son emerge from the shadows as if from the grave had thawed the frozen well of sorrow.

She sobbed, "I thank the gods that they have given me back my son."

"If the gods are so wonderful why did they kill your other two children?" asked Miran sourly. "And why did they kill my Clansmen, and why did they smash by *Bird?* Why . . . ?"

"Shut up!" said Green. "This is no time to cry about anything. We have to get out with whole hides. The philosophizing and tears can come later."

"Mennirox is an ungrateful god," muttered Miran. "After all I did for him, too."

Amra dried her tears and said, "How did you escape? I thought all the males who hadn't been killed in the wreck were speared?"

"Almost everybody was," replied Grizquetr. "But I crawled down into the hold and slipped through to a hiding place beneath one of the fish tanks, which had overturned. It was wet there, and there were dead fish nestling beside me. The savages did not find me, though doubtless they would have when they began salvaging. It was thinking about that that decided me to crawl back out on the other side of the 'roller away from the savages. I did so, and I found that I could belly my way through the grass growing on the edge. I almost died of fright, though, because I crawled head on into Miran. He was hiding there, too."

"I was thrown off the foredeck by the impact," interrupted the captain. "I should have broken every bone in my body, but I landed on a hull sail, which had come down and was lying on the starboard side, supported by the fallen mast. It was like falling into a hammock. From there I dropped into the grass and snaked along the very edge of the island. Several times I almost fell off, and I would have if I'd been a pound fatter, an inch wider. As it was..."

"Listen," said Grizquetr, breaking in. "This island is the *wuru!*"

"What do you mean?" said Green.

"While I was clinging to the edge of the island I thought I'd hang down over it and see if there was any place there to hide. There wasn't, because the underside of the island is one smooth sheet. I know, because I could see in the moonlight clear to the other side. It was smooth, smooth, like a slab of iron.

"And that's not all! You know how the grass on the plains hereabouts has been tall, uncut? Well, the grass just ahead of the edge was uncut. But the grass underneath the island was being cut off. Rather, it was vanishing! The top of the grass was just disappearing into air! Only a lawn of grass about an inch high was left!"

"Then this island *is* one big lawnmower," said Green. "More than just interesting. But we'll have to investigate that later. Right now..."

And he walked toward the little hut by the cave mouth. As he approached it several large house cats streaked out of the doorway. A moment later Green came out. He grinned broadly.

"The priestess has passed out. The place smells like a brewery. The cats are in their cups, too. All drinking from bowls set on the ground for them, staggering around, yowling, fighting. If they don't wake her up, nothing can."

"I have heard that these old priestesses are often drunkards," said Amra. "They lead a lonely life because they're taboo, and nobody even goes near them except during certain religious customs. They have only their bottle and their cats to keep them company."

"Ah," said Miran, "you are thinking of the Tale of Samdroo, the Tailor Who Turned Sailor. Yes, that is supposed to be a story to entertain children, but I'm beginning to think there is a great deal to it. Remember, the story describes just such a hill and just such a cave. It is said that every roaming island has just such a place. And . . ."

"You talk too much," broke in Aga harshly. "Let's get on into the cave."

Green could appreciate what Aga's comment meant. Miran had lost face because he'd allowed his vessel to be wrecked and his Clansmen murdered en masse. To Aga and the other women he was no longer Captain Miran, the rich patriarch. He was Miran, the shipwrecked sailor. A fat old sailor. Just that. Nothing more.

He could have redeemed himself if he had committed suicide. But his eagerness to live had resulted in his placing himself on an even lower level in their estimation.

Miran must have realized this, for he did not reply. Instead he stood to one side.

Green walked thirty paces into the cave, then looked back over his shoulder. The entrance was still visible, an arch outlined in the bright moonshine.

Someone coughed. Green was about to caution them to keep quiet, when he felt his nostrils tickling and had to fight to down a loud sneeze himself.

"Dust."

"Good," said Green. "Maybe they never come down here."

Suddenly the tunnel turned at right angles, to the left. The little light that penetrated from the entrance disappeared in total blackness. The party halted.

"What if there are traps set for intruders?" wailed Inzax.

"That's a chance we'll have to take," Green growled. "We'll go in the dark until we come to another turn. Then we'll light up a torch or two. The natives won't be able to see the glow."

He walked ahead feeling the wall with his left hand. Suddenly he stopped. Amra bumped into him.

"What is it?" she asked anxiously.

"The rock wall has now become metal. Feel here."

He guided her hand.

"You're right," she whispered. "There's a definite seam, and I can tell the difference between the two!"

"The floor's metal, too," added Soon. "My feet are bare, and I can feel it. What's more, the dust is all gone."

Green went ahead, and after thirty more paces he came to another ninety-degree turn, to the right. The walls and floor were composed of the smooth, cool metal. After making sure that the entire party was around the corner, he told a woman carrying some torches taken from a long house to light one. Its bright flare showed the group staring round-eyed at the large chamber in which they stood.

Everywhere were bare gray metal walls and floors. No furniture of any kind.

Nor a speck of dust.

"There's a doorway to another room," he said. "We might as well go on in."

He took the torch from the woman and, holding a cutlass in the other, he led the way. Once across the threshold he halted.

This room was even larger than the other. But it had

furnishings of a sort. And its further wall was not metal but earth.

At the same time the room began to brighten with light coming from an invisible source.

Soon screamed and threw herself against her mother, clinging desperately to her waist. The babies began howling, and the other adults acted in the various ways that panic affected them.

Green alone remained unmoved. He knew what was happening, but he couldn't blame the rest for their behavior. They had never heard of an electronic eye, so they couldn't be expected to maintain coolness.

The only thing that Green feared at that moment was that the outcries would be heard by the savages outside the cave. So he hastened to assure the women that this phenomenon was nothing to be frightened about. It was common in his home country. A mere matter of white magic that anyone could practice.

They quieted down but were still uneasy. Wide-eyed, they bunched up about him.

"The natives themselves aren't scared of this," he said. "They must come here at times. See? There's an altar built against that dirt wall. And from the bones piled beneath it I'd say that sacrifices were held here."

He looked for another door. There seemed to be none. He found it hard to believe that there couldn't be. Somehow he'd had the feeling that great things lay ahead of him. These rooms, and this lighting, were evidences of an earlier civilization that quite possibly had been on a level with his own. He'd known that the island itself must be powered with an automatically working anti-gravity plant, fueled either atomically or from the planet's magneto-gravitic field. Why the whole unit should be covered with rocks and soil and trees he didn't know. But he had been sure that somewhere in the bowels of this mass of land was just such a place as this. And more. Where was the power plant? Was it sealed up so that no one could get to it? Or, as was likely, was there a door to the plant which could not be opened unless one had a key of some sort?"

First he had to find the door.

He examined the altar, which was made of iron. It was a platform about three feet high and ten feet square. Upon it stood a chair, fashioned from pieces of iron. From its back rose a steel rod about half an inch in diameter and ten feet long, its lower end held secure between two uprights by a thick iron fork. Once the fork was withdrawn, the rod would obviously fall over against the earth wall behind it, though the lower end would still remain on the uprights and would, in fact, stick against whoever was sitting in the chair at the moment.

"Odd," said Green. "If it weren't for those catheaded idols on the ends of the platform, and the bones at its foot, I'd not know this *was* an altar. Bones! They're black, burned black."

He looked again at the rod. "Now," he said, half to himself, "if I were to withdraw the fork, and the rod fell, it would strike the wall. That is evident. But what is it all about?"

Amra brought him some long pieces of rope.

"These were stacked against the wall," she said.

"Yes? Ah! Now, if I were to tie one end of this rope about the apex of that rod, and someone else were to stand upon the altar and take out the fork, then I could control which direction the rod would fall by pulling it toward me. Or allowing it to go away from me. And the person who had taken the fork out would then have plenty of time to get down from the altar and back to the region of safety, where the rope-wielder and his friends would be stationed. Alas, the poor fellow sitting in the chair! Yes, I see it all now."

He looked up from the rope he held in his hand. "Aga!" he said sharply. "Get away from that wall!"

The tall, lean woman was walking past the altar, holding her bare cutlass in her hand. When she heard Green she paused in her stride, gave him an astonished look, then continued.

"You don't understand," she called back over her shoulder. "This wall isn't solid earth. It's fluffy, like a young chick's feathers. It's dust, dust. I think we can knock it down, cut our way through. There must be something on the other side. . . ."

"Aga!" he yelled. "Don't! Stop where you are!"

But she had lifted her blade and brought it down in a hard stroke that was to show him how easy the stuff would be to slash away.

Green grabbed Amra and Paxi and dived to the floor, pulling them with him.

Thunder roared and lightning filled the room, dazzling and deafening him! Even in its midst he could see the dark figure of Aga, transfixed, crucified in white fire.

19

THEN AGA was blotted out by the dense cloud of dust that billowed out over her and filled the whole room. With it came an intense heat. Green opened his mouth to cry out to Amra and Paxi to cover their faces and especially their noses. Before he could do so his own open mouth was packed with dust and his nostrils were full. He began sneezing and coughing explosively, while his eyes ran tears in their efforts to wash out the dirt that caked and burned them. Clods of dirt struck him, hurled by the blast. They didn't hurt because they were so small and so fluffy. But they fell so swiftly and in such numbers that he was half-buried under them. Even in the midst of his shock he couldn't help being thankful that he'd been breathing out when the heat struck him. Otherwise he'd have sucked in air that would have seared his lungs, and he'd have dropped dead. As it was, wherever his skin had not been covered by cloth he felt as if he were suffering a bad case of sunburn.

Painfully, he rose on all fours and began crawling toward the other room, where he thought the dust would not be so thick. At the same time he tugged at Amra's arm—at least he supposed it was her arm, since she'd been so close to him when the explosion took place. His gesture was intended to tell her that she should follow him. She rose and followed him, touching him from time to time. Once she stopped, and he turned to find out what was bothering her, even if he felt that he couldn't stand much more of the almost solid dust in his lungs and had to get out to open air or strangle. Then he knew that the woman was Amra, for she was carrying a child in her arms. The child had a scarf around her head and, as he remembered, Paxi was the only infant so dressed.

Coughing violently, he rose to his feet, pulling Amra to hers, and swiftly walked toward where he hoped the exit was. He knew he'd fallen on his face in the general direction of the doorway; if he kept in a straight line he might make it without wandering off to one side.

He found soon enough that he was going just opposite, for he fell headlong over a body on the floor. When he got up again, he ran his hands over the body. The skin was crusty, scaly. Aga's burned corpse. The cutlass was lying by her side, assuring him of her identity.

Reoriented, he turned back, still pulling Amra by the hand. This time he ran into a wall, but he had his free hand stretched out in front of him for just such an event. Frantically, he groped to his left until he came to the corner of the room. Then, knowing that the doorway lay back to his right, he turned and felt along the metal until he came to the opening. He plunged through it, almost fell into the other room, which was as dark and dusty as the one he'd just left. He trotted on ahead, bumped into another wall, groped to his right, found the next exit and ran through that. Here the air was much more free of dust. He could actually make out outlines of his companions as the light was penetrating the fainter haze.

Nevertheless he and the others were coughing and weeping as if they were trying to eject lungs and eyeballs alike. Spasm after spasm shook them.

Green decided that this room wasn't really much better than the others, so he led Amra and Paxi around the right-angled corner and into the dark tunnel. Here his violent rackings began to quiet down and by rapid blinking, which forced tears, he cleaned his eyes of much of the dust. Anxiously, he peered down the passageway toward its end, where the cave mouth formed a dim arch in the moonlight outside.

It was as he'd feared. Somebody stood there, outlined in the beams, bent forward, peering in.

He thought that it must be the priestess, for the figure was slight and the hair was pulled up on top of the head in a great Psyche knot with a feather stuck through it. Moreover, around her feet were four or five cats.

His coughing betrayed him, for the priestess suddenly whirled and trotted off on her sticklike legs. Green dropped Amra's hand and ran, at the same time drawing his stiletto from his belt, as he'd lost his cutlass during the explosion. He had to stop the priestess, though he didn't know what good it would do. The savages sooner or later would come to the sanctuary to ask if she'd seen any of the refugees. And if they couldn't find her they would at once suspect what had happened. The chances were that they already knew. Surely, the noise of the blast must have penetrated even to their ears.

Or had it? The air waves had to round several perpendicular turns before reaching the cave mouth, and it might be that the noise had seemed much greater to Green than it actually was because he'd been so close to it. Perhaps there was some hope.

He ran into the clearing before the cave mouth. The sun was just coming over the horizon, so he could see things clearly. The old woman was nowhere in sight. The only live things were several drunken cats. One of these began to rub its back against Green's leg and purred loudly. Automatically, he stooped down and caressed it, though his gaze flickered everywhere for a sign of the priestess. The door of her hut was open and since it was so small he could be certain that she had no room in there to hide from him. She must have run off down the path.

If so, she wasn't making any noise about it. There were no outcries from her to call her companions to her help.

He found her lying face down on the path, halfway down the hill. At first he thought she was playing possum, so he turned her over, his stiletto ready to shut off any outcry. A glance at her hanging jaw and ashen color convinced him that her possum-playing days were over. At first, he thought she'd tripped and broken her neck, but an examination disproved this. The only thing he could think of was that her old heart had given away under the sudden fright and the stress of running.

Something brushed his ankles. So startled was he, so convinced that a spear had just missed him, he leaped into the air and whirled around. Then he saw that it was only the cat that had rubbed itself against him when he'd first come out of the tunnel. It was a large female cat with a beautiful long black silky coat and with golden eyes. It exactly resembled the Earth cat and was probably descended from the same ancestors as its terrestrial counterpart. Wherever Homo sapiens of the unthinkably long ago had penetrated he seemed to have taken his canine and feline pets.

"You like me, huh?" said Green. "Well, I like you, too, but I'm not going to if you keep on scaring me. I've been through enough tonight for a lifetime."

The cat, purring, paced delicately toward him.

"Maybe you can do me some good," he said and lifted the cat to his shoulder, where she crouched, vibrating with contentment.

"I don't know what you see in me," he confided softly to her. "I must be a frightful-looking object, what with being covered with dust, and my eyes red and raw and running. But then, you're not so delightful yourself, what with your beery breath blowing in my face. I like you very much, What's-your-name. What *is* your name? Let's call you Lady Luck. After all, when I rubbed you I found the priestess dead. If she hadn't died she'd have got away to warn the cannibals. And obviously, you, her luck, had deserted her for me. So Lady Luck it will be. Let's go back up the hill and see what's happened to the rest of my friends."

He found Amra sitting down at the cave's mouth, cuddling Paxi in an effort to quiet her. Nine others were there, too, Grizquetr, Soon, Miran, Inzax, three women, two little girls. The rest, he presumed, were lying dead or unconscious in the altar room. They made a dirty-looking, red-eyed, weary group, not good for much except lying down and passing out.

"Look," he said, "we have to have sleep, whatever else happens. We'll go back into the first chamber and get some there, and . . ."

As one, the others protested that nothing would get them to return anywhere near that horrible fiend-haunted room. Green was at a loss. He thought he knew exactly what had happened, but he just could not explain to these people in terms they'd understand. And they probably would have a dark distrust of him from then on.

He decided to take the simple, if untrue, explanation.

"Undoubtedly Aga provoked a host of demons by striking at the wall behind the altar," he said. "I tried to warn her. You all heard me. But those demons won't bother us again, for we are now under the protection of the cat, the cannibals' totem. Moreover it is the nature of such beings that, once they've released their fury and taken some victims, they are harmless, quiescent, for a long time after. It takes time for them to build up strength enough to hurt human beings again."

They swallowed this offering as they would never have his other explanation.

"If you will lead the way," they said, "we will return. We put our lives in your hands."

Before going into the cave he paused to take another survey. From his spot in the clearing, which was almost on the top of the hill, he could look over the tree tops and see most of the island, except where other hills barred his view. The island had stopped moving and had settled down against the plain itself. Now, to the untutored eye, the entire mass looked like a clump of dirt, rocks and vegetation for some reason rising from the grassy seas. It would remain so until dusk, when it would again launch itself upon its five-mile-an-hour journey to the east. And once having reached a certain point there, it would reverse itself and begin its nocturnal pilgrimage toward the west. Back and forth, shuttling for how many thousands of years? What was its purpose, and whom had its builders been? Surely they could not have conceived in their wildest dreams of its present use, a mobile fortress for a tribe of cannibals?

Nor could they have seen to what uses their dust-collectors would be put. They couldn't have guessed that, millennia thence, men ignorant of their originally intended purpose would be using the devices as part of their religious ritual and of human sacrifice.

Green left the others in the room next to the one where the explosion had taken place. They lay down on the hard floor and at once went to sleep. He, however, felt that there were certain things that had to be done and that he was the only one physically capable of doing them.

20

THOUGH HE HATED to go back into the altar room, he forced himself. The scene of carnage was bad enough, but not as repulsive as he'd expected. Dust had thrown a gray veil of mercy over the bodies. They looked like peaceful gray statues; most of them had not burned on the outside but had died because they'd breathed the first lung-scorching wave of air directly. Nevertheless, despite the look of peace and antiquity, the odor of burned flesh from Aga hung heavy. Lady Luck bristled and arched her back, and for a moment Green thought she was going to leap from his shoulder and run away.

He said, "Take it easy," then decided that she must have smelled this often before. Her present reaction was based on past episodes; probably, there had been great excitement then. The cats, being taboo animals, must have been figures of some importance in the sacrificial ceremonies.

Cautiously, the man approached the wall of dirt behind the altar, even though he did not think there would be any danger for some time to come. The altar itself was comparatively undamaged. Surprised at this, he ran his hand over it and found out that it was composed of baked clay, hard as rock. The chair and metal rod had not been torn loose. Both were tightly bolted down with huge studs which he supposed had been taken off wrecked 'rollers.

The victims that were tied in the chair by the savages must have been sitting looking at the audience, so that their backs were to the wall itself. That meant that when the rod was dropped to make contact between the wall and victim, the discharge only burned the sacrifice's head. Evidence of that was the fact that only skulls were stacked around the altar. The charred head was severed and the body carted outside to one destination or another.

What puzzled Green was how the audience managed to escape the fury of the blast and of the dust, even if they stood at the farthest end of the big room. Determined to find out what happened at those times, he returned to the doorway. Just around its corner, in the second room, he discovered what he'd not noticed before, probably because it was placed so upright and so firmly against one side of the wall. And because its back, which was turned away from the wall, was also made of gray metal. When he switched it around so he could see its other side, he was staring into a mirror about six feet high and four feet wide.

Now he could visualize the ceremony. The victim was strapped into the chair and a rope was tied around the rod. Everybody but the priestess, or whoever conducted the rites, retreated from the altar room. The conductor himself, or herself, then stood in the doorway and released the cord. Before the rod could make contact, the conductor had stepped around the corner. And there the audience saw in the mirror, placed in the doorway so it reflected the interior of the altar room, the ravening discharge of a tremendous electrostatic blast. And immediately afterward, no doubt, they saw nothing because of the dust that would fill the two rooms.

Strange and strong magic to the savages. What myths they must have built about this room, what tales of horrible and powerful gods or demons imprisoned in that wall of dirt! Surely their old women must whisper to the wide-eyed children stories of how the Great Cat-Spirit had been caught by their legendary strong man and savior, some analog to Hercules or Gilgamesh or Thor, and how the Cat-Spirit was the tribe's to keep prisoner with their magic and to appease from time to time with human kills from other tribes lest it become so angry it burst through the wall of earth and devour everybody upon the floating island!

Green knew that it was hopeless to try to dig through that wall, even if it would be safe for days. It might only be several feet thick, or it might be twenty or more.

But however thick it was, he bet that anybody who had the tools, time and strength to excavate would find, embedded somewhere in that mass, several large dust-collectors. He didn't know what shape they'd take, because that would depend on the culture that had built them, and their tastes in decorations would differ from Green's multimillennia-later society. But if they had architectural ideas similar to present-day Terrans they would have constructed the collectors in the shape of busts or of animals' heads or even of bookcases with false backs of books filling them, books that would in reality have been both chargers and filters. The busts or books would have been pierced with many tiny holes, and through these holes the charged particles of dust would have drifted. Once inside the collectors, they would have been burned.

Looking at the blank dirt before him, Green could see what had happened through the ages. Some part of the burning mechanism had gone wrong—as was the custom of mechanisms everywhere. But the charging effect had continued. And though the dust had piled up around the collectors, the extraordinarily powerful fields had continued to work even through the thick blanket. In the beginning, of course, their field could not have caused any human being harm. But these batteries must have been built to adjust to whatever demand was made of them, though their builders, of course, could have had no idea of how great that demand would some day be. Nevertheless it had come, and the batteries had been equal to it. By the time the savages had found this room they were blocked off by this imposing wall.

Through the death of their fellows they had discovered that touching the wall caused a terrible discharge of electrostatic electricity. The rest of the apparatus for execution and the ritual that went with it was foregone and logical, religiously speaking.

Green swore with frustration. How he would love to get through that dirt before another charge built up! On the other side must be another doorway, and it must lead to the fuel and control rooms for this whole island. If he could get inside and there figure out the controls, he'd turn this island upside down and shake off the man-eating monsters. There'd be no holding him then!

He remembered the story of Samdroo, the Tailor Who Turned Sailor. The legend went that Samdroo, his 'roller wrecked upon just such a roaming island as this one, had wandered into just such a cave and through rooms like these. But he'd found no barrier of electrically charged dirt and had walked into a room which contained many strange things. One of them was a great eye that allowed Samdroo to see in it what was happening outside the cave. Another was a board which contained many round faces over which raced little squiggles and lines. Of course, the story had its own explanations for what these things were, but Green could hardly fail to recognize TV, oscilloscopes and other instruments.

Unfortunately his knowledge was going to do him no good. He wasn't going to get through the dirt. Nor was he to be allowed time for excavation and exploration. Every minute on this island meant that he was traveling back to Quotz and its revengeful Duchess and getting farther from Estorya, where the two spacemen and their ship were. He had to find a way of getting off this place and onto some means of transportation.

He left the death chamber and went into the next room. After slumping down against the wall, between Amra with Paxi in her arms, and Inzax with Grizquetr in hers, he chewed some dried meat. Lady Luck meowed for some and he gladly gave her all she wanted. When he'd swallowed all he could hold without bursting and had washed that down with great drafts of the warm and sweet beer taken from the priestess's hut, he closed his eyes. Now, it was up to his Vigilante to take the food and rebuild his wasted tissue, throw off the effects of autointoxication, tone his tired muscles, relax his too-taut nerves, readjust his hormonal balance . . .

21

GREEN DREAMED that his mouth and nose were clogged with dirt and that he was suffocating. He woke to find that, while there was no earth upon him, he was having a difficult time getting his breath. Remedying that by removing the cat from his face, he rose.

"What do you want?" he asked her. She was mewing and striking gently at him.

She padded toward the doorway to the outside, so he imagined that she wished him to follow her. Grasping his cutlass, he walked after her and out to the tunnel that led to the cave mouth. Not until then did he hear the booming of cannon, far away.

The cat meowed plaintively. Evidently, she'd heard cannonfire before and had not liked the results.

Once out of the cave he stopped to look up at the sun.

It was on its downward path from the zenith. About four o'clock in the afternoon. He'd slept about ten hours.

Unable to see much from where he stood, he climbed up the rocks outside the cave and soon stood upon the very top of the hill, a little tableland about ten feet square. From there he commanded as good a view of the island as anyone could get.

Tacking around the periphery of the island were three long, low, black-hulled 'rollers with over-large wheels and scarlet sails. Occasionally a lance of red spurted from one of the vessel's ports, a boom reached Green's ears a few seconds later and he would see the iron ball climb up and up, then fall toward the village. A tree around the clearing would lose a limb, or a spurt of dust would show where a ball landed in the clearing itself. Two of the long houses had big holes in their roofs. The village itself was deserted, as no one with good sense would have remained there. None of the cannibals were visible, but that wasn't surprising, considering how thick the woods were.

Green hoped the Vings would land soon and clean out the savages. That would leave him and his party a clear field, unless the pirates investigated the cave in the same day. If they didn't, then the refugees could leave the island and take to the plains under cover of the night.

Anxiously, Green traced the path that led from the hilltop where he stood and wound down to the village. It was a narrow trail and he often lost sight of it. But always there was a difference in the shading of the tree tops along the trail and the rest of the forest. With his eye he could follow the shading to the village and beyond, toward the back or western part of the island.

It was here that he came across the first sign of hope he had had since the wreck of the *Bird of Fortune*. It was a small break in the vegetation, which ran uninterrupted to the very edge of the island, a shelf of seemingly smooth earth, almost hidden from him by the slope of the terrain. Indeed, he could barely make it out and might have missed it altogether, but he saw the masts of three small 'rollers projecting from above the slope and followed them down toward the hulls. All three were yachts, obviously not of islander make. Beyond the stolen craft were the uprights of davits. These were behind a wall of branches, camouflage for anybody outside the island but visible to those on the inside.

It was all Green could do to keep from whooping with joy. Now he and his party wouldn't have to cast themselves on foot on the dangerous plains. They could sail in comparative safety. Now, while the cannibals were cowering helplessly under the bombardment Green could lead his people through the woods to the yachts. When dusk came and the island began moving again they could lower a yacht from the davits and set sail.

He went back to the cave entrance, where he found everybody awake, waiting for him.

He told them what he'd seen and added, "If the Vings come aboard we'll take advantage of the confusion and escape."

Miran looked at the sun and shook his head. "The Vings won't attack now. It's too close to dusk. They'll want a full day for fighting. They'll follow the island tonight. When dawn comes and the island stops they'll board."

"I bow to your superior experience," Green said. "Only I'd like to ask you one thing. Why don't the Vings launch their small craft at night and land boarding parties from them?"

Miran looked surprised. "No one does that! It's unthinkable! Don't you know that at night the plains abound in spirits and demons? The Vings wouldn't think of taking a chance on what the magic of the savages might unloose against them in the darkness."

"I knew of the general attitude, but it had slipped my mind," admitted Green. "But if this is so, why did you all wander about this place the night the *Bird* was wrecked?"

"That was a situation where we preferred the somewhat uncertain possibility of stumbling across demons to the certainty of being killed by the cannibals," said Miran.

"To be honest," said Amra, "I was too scared to think of ghosts. If I had I might have stayed where I was.... No, I wouldn't either. I've never seen a ghost, but I had seen those savages."

"Well," said Green, "all of you might as well make up your mind that, come ghosts, demons, or men, we're walking through the dark tonight. All those too scared will have to stay behind."

He began issuing orders, and in a short time he had the sleepy-eyed, bedraggled and dirty-looking party ready. After that, he turned to watch the bombardment.

By then it had largely ceased. Only occasionally did one of the vessels loose a single cannon shot. The rest of the time they spent in tacking back and forth and in running up close to the very edge of the island.

"I think they are trying the temper of the island's inhabitants," Green said. "They don't know whether the woods conceal a hundred savages or a thousand, or whether they're armed with cannons and muskets or just with spears. They want to draw fire, so they can get an estimate of what they're facing."

He turned to Miran. "Which reminds me, why is it that the natives don't use guns? They must have a chance to get their hands on many from the wrecks."

The fat merchant shrugged and rolled his one good eye to indicate that he didn't really know but was making a guess.

"Probably they've a taboo against using firearms. Whatever the reason, they're evidently suffering because they neglect them. Look how few they are. Only fifty men! They must have lost quite a few through raids from other savage tribes, both from those who live upon the plain itself and from those who live on other roaming islands. They're down to the point now where they must die out within a generation, even without help from such as those," he said, pointing to the Ving 'rollers.

"Yes, and I suppose that during the daytime, when the island is stopped, grass cats and dire dogs board it. These must take their toll of the humans."

He gazed again at the red sails and wheels of the Vings. "I'd think that those pirates would take every island they could and would use them as bases from which to operate."

"They do," said Amra. "For a generation now the Vings have been scouring the plains, locating the islands and exterminating the savages on them. Then they've fortified the islands, so that you might say that today the Xurdimur is dominated by them. But there's a drawback to an island as a harbor. No large 'roller may get very close except in the daylight. They have to put out to grass every night and follow their base at a safe distance until dawn. However, though the Vings are well established on many roamers, they're often attacked by the navies of various nations and sometimes driven off. Then the nation that takes possession of the island has a nice little base. And, of course, quite often they use it to launch their own piratical ventures against the craft of countries at peace with them.

"Oh, the Xurdimur is a land where every man's hand is against the other, and the devil take the ones with short sail! A man may make his fortune or break his heart, all in a night's work. But, then, you know that only too well."

Green interrupted, "We'll leave them, and the natives, too, when moonlight gets here. I only hope that there aren't other Ving craft in the neighborhood."

"What the gods will, happens," replied Miran. His sad

face reflected the belief that if he, the favorite of Mennirox, could come to grief, then Green could expect even worse.

When dusk came, Green walked from the cave into the dark and hard rain. Behind him came Amra, one hand upon his shoulder, the other supporting Paxi. The rest were stretched out in a line behind her, each person's hand on the shoulder of the one ahead.

The black cat was underneath Green's coat, riding in a large pocket of his shirt. She had made it plain to him that where he went, she went. And Green, to avoid a big fuss and also because he was beginning to feel very affectionate toward her, allowed her to come along.

The descent from the hilltop was an anxious and stumbling trip. Green, after ten minutes of groping along the path, had to acknowledge he did not know where he was. So many windings had the path taken that he did not know whether he was going east, north, south, or in the right direction, west.

Actually, it didn't really matter, as long as it brought him to the edge of the island. He could skirt the edge until he arrived at the fleet craft that would give them a chance for flight.

The trouble was in finding that rim. He was afraid that it would be possible to wander in circles and figure eights until moonlight. Then, though they'd be able to orient themselves, they'd also be exposed to the view of the cannibals. And if they found themselves, say, at the eastern edge, their journey around would be perilous indeed.

Occasional lightning flashed, and then he could make out his immediate environment. These brief revelations weren't much help. All he could see were the solid-seeming walls of tree trunks and bushes.

Suddenly Amra spoke. "Do you think we're getting close?"

He stopped so suddenly that the entire line lurched into

him. Lightning burst again, quite close by. The cat, curled in his coat pocket, spat and tried to shrink into an even smaller ball. Absently, Green patted her from outside the coat. He said, "Your name *is* Lady Luck. I just saw the village. Now we're getting some place. I really needed that referent."

He wasn't worried about the inhabitants of the village. All were undoubtedly cowering under the roofs of their long houses, praying to whatever gods they worshiped that they would not send the lightning their way. There would be little danger if the whole party were to walk through the center of the village. He planned to take no chances at all, however, and ordered everybody to follow him around the clearing.

"It won't be long now!" he said to Amra. "Pass the word back and cheer everybody up."

Half an hour later he wished he'd kept his mouth shut. It was true that he'd followed the wandering path to the cove where their boats were kept. But he'd at once drawn his breath in pain of surprise.

A lightning bolt had illuminated the gray rock wall of the cove, its broad shelf, and the high black iron davits.

But the yachts were gone!

22

LATER GREEN THOUGHT that if ever the time came when he should have cracked up, that instant of loss, white and sudden as the lightning itself, should have been the one.

The others cried out loudly in their grief and shock, but he was as silent as the empty stone shelf. He could not move nor utter a word; all seemed hopeless, so what was the use of motion or talk?

Nevertheless, he was human, and human beings hope even when there is no justification for it. Nor could he remain frozen until the next stroke of lightning would reveal to the others the state of their leader. He *had* to act. What if his actions *were* meaningless? Mere movement answered for the demands of the body, and at that moment it was his body that could move. His mind was congealed.

Shouting to the others to scatter and look about in the

brush, but not to scatter too far, he began climbing up the slope of the hill. When he had reached its top he left the path and plunged into the forest to his right on the theory that if the yachts were anywhere they must be there. He had two ideas about where they might be. One was that the Vings had spotted them and had sent in a party aboard a gig to push them over the side of the island. Thus, when the island had begun its nightly voyage it had left the 'rollers sitting upon the plain. The other theory was also inspired by the presence of the Vings. Perhaps the savages had hidden their craft because of just such an event as his first theory put forth. To do that they would have had to haul the 'rollers up the less steep slant of the cove.

At the point where he would have looped a rope around a tree and used it to pull a yacht uphill, he saw all three of the missing craft. They were nestling side by side just over the lip of the slope, their hulls hidden by brush piled up before them. Their tall masts, of course, would be taken for tree trunks by anybody but a very close observer.

Green yelled with joy, then whirled to run back and tell the others. And slammed into a tree trunk. He picked himself up, swearing because he'd hurt his nose. And tripped over something and fell again. Thereafter, he seemed to be in a nightmare of frustration, of conspiracy between tree and night to catch and delay him. Where his trip up had been easy, his trip back was a continued barking of shins, bumping of nose, and tearing loose from clutching bushes and thorns. His confusion wasn't at all helped when the lightning ceased, because he'd been guiding himself by its frequent flashes. And Lady Luck, alarmed at all the hard knocks she was getting, struggled out of his shirt pocket and slipped into the forest. He called to her to come back, but she had had enough of him, for the time being, anyway.

For a brief moment he thought of the fantastic device of grabbing hold of her tail and following her through the dark.

But she was gone, and the idea wouldn't have worked, anyway. More than likely she'd have turned and bitten his hands until he released her.

There was nothing to do but make his own way back.

After ten minutes of frantic struggling, during which he suddenly realized he'd turned the wrong way and was wandering away from the edge of the island, he saw the clouds disappear. With the bright moon came vision and sanity. He turned around and in a short time was back at the cove.

"What happened to you?" asked Amra. "We thought maybe you'd fallen off the edge."

"That's about all that didn't happen," he said, irritated now that he had been so easily lost. He told them where the yachts were and added, "We'll have to let one down by a rope before we can connect it to the davits. It'll take a lot of pushing and pulling, a lot of muscle. Everybody up on the hill, including the children!"

Wearily, they climbed up the slope to the top and shoved one of the 'rollers up the slight incline of the depression to the lip of the hill. Green picked up one of the wet ropes lying on the ground and passed it around the tree. Its trunk had a groove where many ropes had worn a path during similar operations. One end he gave to half of the party, putting Miran in charge of them. The other end he tied in a bowknot to a huge iron eye which projected from the stern of the craft. Then, ordering the other half of the women to help him push, he got the 'roller over the lip and down the slope, while the rope gang slowly released the double loop around the tree in short jerks.

When the craft had halted by the davits, Green untied the rope. His next step would be to back the yacht in between the davits so that he could hook up its ropes and lift it. Fortunately, there was a winch and cable for this. Unfortunately, the winch was hand-operated and had been allowed to get rusty. It would work only with great resistance and with loud squeaking. Not that more noise mattered, for the party had made so much that only the fact that the wind was from the east could have kept the savages in ignorance of the survivors' whereabouts.

It was as if his thinking of them had brought them upon the scene. Grizquetr, who'd been stationed in a tree as a sentinel, called down, "I see a torch! It's somewhere in the woods, about half a mile away. Oh! There's another one! And another one!"

Green said, "Do you think they're on the path that leads here?"

"I don't know. But they're coming this way, winding here and there, wandering like Samdroo when he was lost in the Mirrored Mazes of Gil-Ka-Ku, The Black One! Yes, they must be on the path!"

Green began feverishly tying the davit-ropes to the axles of the craft. He sweated with anxiety and cursed when his fumbling fingers got in the way of his haste. But the tying of the four bowknots actually took less than a minute, in spite of the way time seemed to race past him.

That done he had to order off the yacht some of the women who had climbed aboard. Only the women who had to take care of very small infants and the older children were to be on that boat.

"Just who do you think is going to work the winch?" he barked at the too-eager. "Now, jump to it!"

One of the women on the 'roller wailed, "Are you going to stay on the island and leave us all alone on this 'roller in the midst of the Xurdimur?"

"No," he answered as calmly as possible. "We're going to lower you to the ground. Then we're going back up the hill and shove the other 'rollers over the edge so that they can't be used by the savages to come after us. We'll jump off and walk back to you."

Seeing that the women were still not convinced and softened by their pitiable looks, he called to Grizquetr.

"Come down! And get on the boat!"

And when the boy had run down the slope and halted by his side, breathing hard and looking up at him for his orders, Green said, "I'm delegating you to guard these women and babies until we arrive. Okay?"

"Okay," said Grizquetr, grinning, his chest swelling because of the importance of the duty. "I'm captain until you climb aboard, is that it?"

"You're a captain and a good one too," said Green, slapping him lightly on the shoulder. Then he ordered the winches turned until the 'roller was hoisted into the air a few inches. As soon as the rusty machines had groaningly fulfilled their functions he had the craft lowered over the edge and down to the plain. The transition was smoothly made; the yacht's wheels began turning; the nose lifted only slightly because of the superior pull on the ropes tied to the bow; the stern ropes were paid out a little to equalize the strain; then, obeying Green's gesture, the women aboard it pulled at the bowknots, which untied simultaneously. Not until then did he breathe a little easier, for if one or more had refused to slip loose as swiftly as another, the craft might have been pulled up on one side or dragged around by either end and thus capsized.

For a few seconds he watched the 'roller slip away, coasting on its momentum but headed at right angles to the direction of the island. Then it had stopped, and it began to grow smaller as the island left it behind. From it came the thin wailing of his daughter, Paxi. It broke the spell that momentarily held him. He began running up the slope, shouting, "Follow me!"

Reaching the crest of the hill ahead of the others, he took time for a glance through the woods. Sure enough, torches bobbed up and down and flickered in and out as they passed between tree trunks. And there were drums beating somewhere on the island.

Lady Luck shot out of the woods, leaped upon Green's knee, scaled his shirt front and came to rest upon his shoulder. "Ah, you wandering wench, you," he said, "I knew you couldn't stay away from my irresistible charm, now could you?"

Lady Luck didn't reply but gazed anxiously at the forest.

"Never fear, my pretty little one," he said. "They'll not touch a hair of my fine blond head. Nor a silky black one of yours."

By then the others, puffing and panting, had gained the top of the hill. He set them to pushing on the stern of a yacht, and in a minute they had sent it headlong down the hill. When it rushed over the edge and disappeared with a crash on the plain below they had all they could do to restrain their cheers. Small revenge for the suffering they'd had to undergo. But it was something.

"Now for the other," said Green. "Then everybody run as if the demons of Gil-Ka-Ku were on your tails!"

Grunting, they pushed the last 'roller up the little incline, then gathered their strength for the final heave that would launch it, too, upon its last voyage.

And at that moment some savages who'd been running ahead of the torch-bearers burst out of the woods.

Green took one look and realized that they would get between the edge of the island and his party. There were about ten of them; they not only outnumbered his own force but were strong men against women. And they had spears, whereas his people were armed mainly with cutlasses.

Green didn't waste any time in meditation. "Everybody aboard except Miran and me!" he said loudly. "Don't argue! Get in! We're riding through them! Lie flat on the deck!"

Screaming, the women scrambled over the low rail and

onto the deck. As soon as the last one was on, the Earthman and Miran put their shoulders to the stern and pushed. For a second it looked as though their combined strength would not be enough, as if the party should have shoved the craft a little further over the lip of the hill before stopping.

"There's not time to get them out again to help us!" panted Green. "Dig in, Miran, get that fat into gear, shove, damn you, shove!"

It seemed to him that he was breaking his own collarbone under the pressure and that he'd never felt such hard and cutting wood in all his life. And it seemed that the 'roller was stubbornly refusing to move until the cannibals arrived in time to save it, like the Marines. His legs quivered, and his intestines, he was sure, were writhing about like snakes, striking here and there against the wall of his belly, seeking a weak place where they might erupt through into the open air and leave this man who subjected them to such toil.

There was a shout from the warriors assembled below and a thud of their feet as they charged up.

"Now or never!" shouted Green.

His face felt like one big blood vessel, and he was sure that he was going to blow his top, literally. But the 'roller moved forward, crept slowly, groaned—or was that he?— and began moving swiftly, too swiftly, down the slope. Too swiftly, because he had to run after it, grab the taffrail and haul himself over. And while he was doing that he had to extend a hand to Miran, who wasn't as fast on his feet.

Fortunately Amra had presence of mind enough to grab Miran by the shoulder of his shirt and help pull. Over the rail he came, crying out in pain as his big stomach burned against the hard mahogany, but not forgetting the bag of jewels clutched in his hand.

Lady Luck had already deserted her post on Green's shoulder when he began pushing. Now she meowed softly and pressed against him, scared at the shaking of the deck and the rumbling of the wheels as the craft sped downhill.

He pulled her to him in the protection of the crook of his arm, and reared up on his elbow to see what he could see. What he saw was a spear flying straight at him. It shot by so close he fancied he could feel the sharp edge of its blade graze him, and there was nothing of his imagination about the woman's scream that rose immediately afterward. It sounded so much like Amra that he was sure she'd been hit; however, he had no time to turn and find out. An islander had appeared by the side of the yacht, and as the deck was on a level with his chest, the fellow could see them all easily enough. His arm flew back, then leaped forward, and the spear he held darted straight at Green.

No, not at him, but at Lady Luck. Another warrior, a little further down the slope, screaming something, also thrust at the cat. Evidently felines were no longer taboo upon this island. The former worshipers considered that their totem had deserted them and therefore deserved death.

Lady Luck, however, had the traditional nine lives. None of the razor sharp blades came very close to her. And in the next few seconds the savages were left howling upon the slope or lying unconscious on the spot where the 'roller had struck them. The vessel sped down the steep incline, bumped hard as it roared out upon the stone shelf, and flew into the air. Green flattened himself out against the deck, hoping thus to dampen the effect of the three-foot drop onto the plain.

Somehow he became separated from the deck, was floating in the air, and saw the planks rushing up at him.

There was a brief interlude of darkness before Green awoke and realized that the meeting of the deck and his face had done the latter no good at all and might have resulted in considerable damage. He was sure of it when he spit out his two front teeth. However, his pain was overwhelmed in the rush of joy at having escaped. For the island was retreating across the flat, moonlit Xurdimur while its inhabitants screamed and jumped with fury and frustration on the rim, unable to bring themselves to leap after the refugees. Home was where the island was, and they weren't going to get left behind for the sake of revenge.

"I hope the Vings exterminate you tomorrow," muttered Green. Wearily and painfully, he rose to his feet and surveyed what was left of the Clan Effenycan. Amra was unhurt. If it was she who'd screamed when the spear had passed over Green, she'd done it from fright. The spear itself was sticking out from the base of the mast, its head half-buried in the wood.

He climbed over the side and inspected the damage done by the three-foot drop. One of the wheels had fallen off, and an axle was bent. Shaking his head, he spoke to the others, "This roller is done for. Let's start walking. We've a boat to catch."

23

TWO WEEKS LATER the yacht was scudding along under a twenty-mile-an-hour wind. It was high noon, and everybody except the helmsmen, Amra and Miran was eating. They were lunching on steaks carved from a *hoober* which Green had shot from the deck and which had been cooked on the fireplace placed under a hood immediately aft of the small foredeck. There was no lack of food despite the fact that the yacht had not been stocked. Fortunately the savages who'd owned it had not bothered to remove the several pistols and the keg of powder and sack of balls from its locker. With this Green killed enough deer and *hoobers* to keep everybody well fed. Amra supplemented their protein diet with grass which her culinary art turned into a halfway decent salad. At times, when they neared a grove of trees, Green would stop the yacht. They would go foraging for berries and for a large plant which could be beaten until soft, mixed with water, kneaded and baked into a kind of bread.

Once, a grass cat dashed out from behind a tree, making straight for Inzax. Green and Miran, both firing at the same time, crumpled it within ten yards of the little blonde.

The grass cats, big cheetah-like creatures with long slim legs built for running, were only a peril when the party left the yacht. Though fully capable of leaping aboard when the 'roller was in movement, they never did. Sometimes they might pace it for a mile or so, then they would contemptuously walk away.

Green wished he could say the same for the dire dogs. These were almost as large as the grass cats and ran in packs of from six to twelve. Sinister-looking with their gray-and-black spotted coats, pointed wolfish ears and massive jaws, they would run up to the very wheels, howling and snapping with their monstrous yellow fangs. Then one would be inspired with the idea of leaping aboard and finding out how the occupants tasted. Up he would come, easily sailing over the railing. Usually the occupants would discourage him with a well-placed thrust from a spear or an amputating swing of a cutlass. Sometimes they missed, and he would land on the deck, which enabled the sailors to try again, with better success. Back over the rail his body would go, back to his fellows, many of whom would stop the chase to devour their dead comrade. Those who persisted in the hunt would then try their luck, bounding upon the yacht, snarling hideously, trying to scare their quarry into a complete paralysis and sometimes succeeding.

No lives were lost to the dire dogs, but almost everybody bore scars. Only Lady Luck managed to stay unscathed. Every time she heard their distant howling she scaled the mast and would not come down until the danger was over.

Today they'd not been bothered. Everybody relaxed,

chattering and munching happily the unexciting but nutritious meat of the *hoober*. Miran stood upon the foredeck, sighting at the sun through his sextant. This also had been found in the locker, along with some charts of the Xurdimur. Though the charts had had their locations marked in an alphabet unknown to anybody aboard, Miran had been able to compare them in his mind to the charts he'd left on the *Bird of Fortune*. He had crossed out the foreign names and put in names in the Kilkrzan alphabet. He'd done this only at the insistence of Green, who didn't trust Miran to translate for him and wanted to be able to read the maps himself. Not only that, he'd forced the fat merchant to teach both him and Amra how to use the clumsy and complicated but fairly accurate sextant.

A few days later, after Green and his wife had begun to study the navigation instrument, there occurred the accident that forced Green to take further measures to safeguard himself. He and Miran had been standing at the stern, ready with their pistols while Amra steered the yacht toward a group of *hoobers*. They were going through their usual maneuver of running down a herd until the exhausted animals could be overtaken. Just as they neared an orange-colored stallion, galloping furiously, Green raised his pistol. At the same time he was vaguely aware that Miran had also sighted but had stepped back, behind and to one side of him. Sensitive about wasting any of the valuable ammunition, Green had turned his head to warn Miran not to shoot unless he, Green, missed. It was then that he saw the muzzle swerving toward the back of his head. He ducked, fully expecting to get his brains blown out before he could shout a warning. But Miran, seeing his reaction, lowered the muzzle and puzzledly asked Green what he was doing.

Green didn't answer. Instead he took the gun away from Miran's limp grip and silently put it away in the locker. Neither he nor the merchant ever referred to the incident, nor did Miran ask why he was not permitted to take part in any shooting thereafter. That convinced Green that the fellow had fully intended to shoot him. And then claim to the others that it had been an accident.

To forestall any more attempts at "accidents" Green told Amra that if he were to disappear some dark night, she was to see that a certain person was shot and thrown overboard. He did not name the certain person, but he mentioned his sex and as Miran was the only other man on the yacht, there was no doubt about to whom he referred. Thereafter, Miran was most cooperative, always smiling and joking. However, Green caught him now and then with frowning brows and a thoughtful expression. He was either fingering his stiletto or the bag of jewels he carried inside his shirt. Green could imagine that he was planning something for the day they reached Estorya.

Now, on this day two weeks after they'd left the island, Miran was shooting the sun, and Green was waiting until he was through, so he could check on him. If his calculations were correct the yacht should be directly east of Estorya two hundred miles. If they maintained their average rate of twenty-five miles an hour they'd reach the windbreak in a little over eight hours.

The fat merchant quit looking through the eyepiece of his instrument and walked to the cockpit where his charts and papers were. Green took the sextant from him and made his own observations, then checked with Miran in the narrow and crowded cockpit.

"We agree," said Green, indicating with the pencil tip a round scarlet spot on the chart. "We should be sighting this island within four hours."

"Yes," replied Miran. "That is an old landmark. It has been there a hundred miles due east of Estorya since before my grandfather's time. It was once a roaming island, but it long ago quit moving and has stayed in that one spot. That is nothing unusual. Every captain knows of these fixed islands scattered all over the Xurdimur, and every now and then we have to add a new red mark to our charts because one of the roamers has settled down."

He paused, then added a statement that set Green's heart to beating fast.

"The unusual thing about this island is that it did not stop of its own accord. It was halted by the magic of the Estoryans, and it has been kept in that one place ever since by their magic."

"What do you mean?" asked Green eagerly.

Miran's round, pale-blue eye stared at him blankly.

"What do you mean what do I mean? I mean just what I said, nothing more."

"I mean, what magic did they contrive to halt this roamer?"

"Why, they put up certain peculiar towers in its path, and when the island began going backwards to get out of the trap and go around it, they moved other towers to block its retreat. These towers moved fast on many well-greased wheels. Once the circle was completed the island couldn't move. Nor has it been able to move since."

"These towers intrigue me. How did the Estoryans know how to halt these islands? And if they've succeeded with one, why not with the others?"

"I do not know. Perhaps because the towers are huge and costly and don't move too fast. Perhaps it is not worthwhile to the Estoryans to capture many. As for their knowledge, I think they got it from their ancestors. It was their great-great-great-and-then-some-grandfathers who originally built Estorya in the middle of the plain and protected it from being crushed by these islands by placing these many towers all around their city. But it cost them much wood and time, and perhaps they lost interest after that."

Miran indicated a castle inked in beside the red spot.

"That castle means that a military or naval fortification

has been built there on the island. It is the furtherest eastern garrison of the Estoryans. When we come within sighting distance of it we are supposed to report. Of course, if you wish to avoid it, we may sail to the north or south and swing around it. But then we will have to report to the windbreak master of the city itself, and they are rather hostile to captains who have failed to have their papers checked at the fort of Shimdoog. Even if the craft is such a small and weak one as this. The Estoryans are a suspicious people."

Yes, thought Green, and I'll bet that you intend to inflate their distrust with certain information about me.

He rose from the cockpit, and at the same time he heard Amra hail him from her station at the helm.

"Island on the horizon," she said. "And many glittering white objects placed before it."

Green refrained from comment. But he had a hard time concealing his excitement, which grew with every turn of the wheels. He paced back and forth, stopping now and then to shade his eyes and look long at the white towers. Finally, as they got so near that he could no longer be mistaken about their size or the details of their peculiar structure, he could contain himself no longer.

He whooped with joy and kissed Amra on the cheek and danced around and around the foredeck while the women stared with embarrassment and concern and the children giggled, all wondering if he'd gone mad.

"Spaceships! Spaceships!" he howled in English. "Dozens of them! It must be an expedition! I'm saved, saved! Spaceships, spaceships!"

24

THEY WERE A MAGNIFICENT sight, those many cones pointing their skyscraping noses upward and their spreading landing struts sinking into the soft earth! Their white eternum metal gleamed in the sun, dazzling the spectator who happened to catch their radiance full in the eyes. They were glorious, embodying all the vast wisdom and skill of the greatest civilization of the Galaxy.

No wonder, thought Green, that I dance and howl while these people look at me as if I'm mad, and Amra, tears in her eyes, shakes her head and says something to herself. What can they know of the meaning of those splendors?

What, indeed?

"Hey," shouted Green, "Hey! Here I am! An Earthman! Maybe I look like one of these barbarians, with my long hair and bushy beard and dirty skin, but I'm not. I'm Alan Green, an Earthman!"

Of course, they couldn't have heard him at that distance, even if somebody had been standing beneath the spaceships to hear him. But he howled with sheer exuberance, not worrying about wasting his breath and making himself hoarse.

Finally Amra interrupted him.

"What is the matter, Alan? Have you been bitten by the Green Bird of Happiness, which sometimes flies over these plains? Or has the White Bird of Terror nipped you while you slept last night upon the open deck?"

Green paused and looked steadily at her. Could he tell her the truth, now he was so near salvation? It was not that he was worried about her or the others stopping him from making contact with the expedition. Nothing could stop him now, he was sure of that.

It was just that he hesitated to tell her that he would be leaving her. The idea of hurting her was agony to him.

He started to speak in English, caught himself, and switched to her language. "Those vessels—they have brought my people from across the space between the stars. I came to this world in just such a vessel, a spaceroller, you might say. My ship crashed, and I was forced to descend upon this—your—world. Then, I heard that another ship had landed near Estorya and that King Raussmig had put the crew in prison and was going to sacrifice them during the Festival of the Sun's Eye. I had little time to get to Estorya before that happened, so I talked Miran into taking me. That was why I left you, that . . ."

He trailed off because he did not understand the expression upon her face. It was not the great hurt he'd expected, nor the wild fury he thought might result from his explanation. If anything, she looked pitying.

"Why, Alan, whatever are you talking about?"

He pointed at the line of spaceships.

"They're from Terra, my home planet."

"I don't understand what you mean by your home planet," she replied still pityingly. "But those are not spaceships. Those are the towers built by the Estoryans a thousand years ago."

"Wha-what do you mean?"

Stunned, he looked at them again. If those weren't starships he'd eat the yacht's canvas. Yes, and the wheels, too.

Under the swift wind, the 'roller swept closer and closer while he stood behind Amra and thought that he'd break into little pieces if his tension didn't find some release.

Finally it did find an outlet. Tears welled in his eyes, and he choked. His breast seemed as if it would swell up and burst.

How cleverly the ancient builders had fashioned those towers! The landing struts, the big fins, the long sweeping lines ending in the pointed nose, all must have been built with a spaceship as a model. There was no escaping such a conclusion; coincidence couldn't explain it.

Amra said, "Don't cry, Alan. Your people will think you weak. Captains don't weep."

"This captain does," he replied, and he turned and walked the length of the yacht to the stern and leaned over the taffrail where no one could see him as he shook with sobs.

Presently he felt a hand upon his.

"Alan," she said gently. "Tell me the truth. If those had been ships on which you could leave this world and travel into the skies, would you have taken me along? Were you still thinking that I was not—not good enough for you?"

"Let's not talk about it now," he said. "I can't. Besides, there are too many people listening. Later, when everybody's asleep."

"All right, Alan."

She released his hand and left him alone, knowing that that was what he wanted. Mentally, he thanked her for it, because he knew what it was costing her to exercise restraint. At any other time, in a like situation, she would have thrown something at him.

After he had calmed down somewhat he returned to the helm and took over from Miran. From then on he was too busy to think much about his disappointment. He had to report to the port officer and tell his story, which took hours, for the officer called in the others to hear his amazing tale. And they questioned Miran and Amra. Green anxiously listened to the merchant's account, fearful that the fellow would disclose his suspicions that Green was not what he claimed to be. If Miran had any such intentions, however, he was saving them for their arrival in Estorya itself.

The officers all agreed that they had heard many wonderful stories from sailors but never anything to match this. They insisted upon giving a banquet for Miran and Green. The result was that Green got a much-needed and desired bath, haircut and shave. But he also had to endure a long feast in which he had to stuff himself to keep from offending his hosts and also was forced to enter a drinking contest with some of the younger blades of the post. His Vigilante could handle enormous amounts of food and alcohol, so that Green appeared to the soldiers to be something of a superman. At midnight the last officer had dropped his head upon the table, dead drunk, and Green was able to get up and go to his yacht.

Unfortunately he had to carry the fat merchant out on his shoulders. Outside the banquet room he found a few rickshaw boys standing around a fire, huddled together, waiting for a customer so drunk he wouldn't fear thieves or ghosts. He gave one of them a coin and told him to deliver Miran to the yacht.

"What about yourself, honored sir? Don't you wish to ride home, too?"

"Later," said Green, looking up past the fort and at the hills behind it. "I intend to take a walk to clear my head."

Before the rickshaw men could question him further he plunged into the darkness and began striding swiftly toward the highest peak upon the island.

Two hours later he suddenly appeared in the moonlight-drenched windbreak, walked past the many vessels tied down for the night and crawled aboard his own yacht. A glance around the deck convinced him that everybody was sleeping. He stepped softly past the prostrate forms and lay down by Amra. Face up, his hands behind his head, he stared at the moon, a thoughtful expression upon his face.

Amra whispered, "Alan, I thought you were going to talk to me tonight."

He stiffened but did not turn his head to look at her.

"I was, but the officers kept us up late. Didn't Miran get here?"

"Yes, about five minutes before you did."

He rose on one elbow and looked searchingly at her. *"What?"*

"Is there anything strange about that?"

"Only that he was so drunk he'd passed out and was snoring like a pig. The fat son of an *izzot!* He must have been faking! And he must have . . ."

"Must have what?"

Green shrugged. "I don't know."

He couldn't tell her that Miran must have followed him up into the hills. And that if he had the fellow must have seen some very disturbing things.

He stood up and gazed intently at the dark forms stretched out here and there. Miran was sleeping upon a blanket behind the helm. Or was pretending to do so.

Should he kill him? If Miran turned him in to the authorities in Estorya . . .

He sat down again and fingered his dagger.

Amra must have guessed his thoughts, for she said, "Why do you want to kill him?"

"You know why. Because he could have me burned."

She sucked her breath in with a hiss.

"Alan, it can't be true! You can't be a demon!"

To him the accusation was so ridiculous that he didn't bother to answer. He should have known better, because he was well aware of how seriously these people took such things. However, he was thinking so furiously about what he could do to forestall Miran, that he completely forgot about her. Not until he heard her muffled sobs did he come out of his reverie. Surprised, he said, "Don't worry. They're not going to burn me."

"No, they're not," she said, choking on every other word. "I don't care if you *are* a demon. I love you, and I'd go to hell for you or with you!"

It took him a few seconds to understand that she did believe he *was* a demon and that it made no difference to her. Or, rather, she was determined to ignore the difference. What a sacrifice of her natural feelings she must have made for him! She, like everybody upon this world, had been trained from childhood to develop a fierce disgust and horror of devils and to be always upon her guard for them when they appeared in human form. What an abyss she had to cross in order to conquer her deep revulsion! In a way, her feat was greater than crossing the chasm between the stars.

"Amra," he said, deeply touched, and he bent down to kiss her.

To his surprise she turned her face away.

"You know my lips don't belch fire, like the devils' in the legends," he said, half-jestingly, half-pityingly. "Nor will I suck your soul into my mouth."

"You have already done that," she said, still not facing him.

"Oh, Amra!"

"Yes, you have! Else why should I follow you when you deserted me to run away on the *Bird?* And why should I still want to follow you, to be with you, even if those towers had turned out to be your what-do-you-call-'em? and you had sailed away into the skies on them? Why would any decent human woman want to do that? Tell me!"

She, too, rose on an elbow, her face now turned to him. He scarcely recognized her, her features were so twisted and her skin was so livid.

"A hundred times during this voyage I've wished you would die. Why? Because then I wouldn't have to think about the time to come when you would leave this world forever, leave *me* forever! But when you were in danger, then I almost died, too, and I knew I didn't really wish your death. It was just wounded pride on my part. And I couldn't face the moment of your departure! Or the fact that you must come from a superior race, a people more like gods than demons!

"Oh, I didn't know what to think! Whether you were a devil, or a god, or just a man who was somehow more of a man than any I knew. I could ignore such things as your wounds healing up faster than they should and scar tissues disappearing. But I couldn't ignore your knowledge that Aga would be killed if she touched that wall in the room on the cannibals' island. Nor the fact that your teeth grew back in after they were knocked out during the escape from the island. Nor your too obvious interest in those two demons held prisoner in Estorya. Or..."

"Not so loud, Amra," he interrupted. "You'll wake everybody up."

"All right, all right. Better to keep quiet and pretend to be stupid. But I can't, I'm not built that way. So... what are you going to do, Alan?"

"Do? Do?" he repeated miserably. "Why, somehow or

other I'm going to free those two poor devils and escape in their spaceship."

"Devils? Then they *are* demons!"

"Oh, no, that was just a manner of speaking. I said poor devils because of what they must have gone through in that barbarous prison. They might as well have been in the hands of the cannibals as at the mercy of the priests of this wretched planet."

"Yes, that's what you really think of us, isn't it? That we're all murderous, dirty and stinking savages."

"Oh, not all of you," he replied. "You're not, Amra. By any standards, you're a wonderful woman."

"Then why can't . . . ?"

She bit her lip and turned away from him. She would not humble herself by asking him to take her with him. It was up to him to make the offer.

Green did not know what to say, though he knew that it was necessary to say something at once.

He just could not make up his mind as to how she would fit into Earth civilization.

How could he teach her that if somebody whom you didn't like differed with you, you just didn't try to tear them apart? Or that if the person you hated was too powerful for you to settle matters with personally you didn't resort to professional assassins?

How could he teach her to love the same things he did, the music and literature of his own culture? Her roots were in an entirely different culture. She couldn't possibly understand what he understood, thrill to that which thrilled him, catch the subtleties that he caught, see what lay behind the nuances of his civilization. She'd be a stranger in a world not made for her.

Of course, he thought, there were plenty of women upon Earth and her star-colonies who didn't share his culture, even if they'd been brought up in it. But their case was simply a matter of taste. And they could still share a certain amount with him, just because they'd breathed the same atmosphere and talked the same words as he. Not that he would have cared to live with them, because he wouldn't. But Amra, desirable in so many ways, just would not understand what was taking place around her or in the minds of those she would have to live with.

He looked down at Amra. Her back was turned, and she seemed to be breathing the easy breath of deep sleep. Though he doubted very much that she could be sleeping, he decided to accept things as they looked. He wouldn't answer her now, though he knew that when morning came her eyes would be asking the same question, even if she didn't voice it.

At least, he thought, she'd been diverted from her curiosity about what he'd been doing that night. That was something. He didn't want anybody to know about that. Not until the time for action came.

Provided, that is, that he could do anything even then. He'd discovered certain things tonight that could mean his salvation if he could utilize them.

That was the rub, as some poet or other had once said.

Wondering just who had originated that saying, he fell asleep. Woolgathering had always been a favorite occupation of his when people left him alone to do it. That was the rub. They didn't.

25

SHORTLY AFTER DAWN the yacht set sail and sped toward
Estorya, a hundred miles west. The breeze was a strong
thirty-five miles an hour, precursor of the violent winds that
roared across the Xurdimur during the rainy season. Green
set every inch of sail he had and took over the helm himself.
Steering was not as simple as it had been, for traffic was
getting heavy. In an hour he saw no less than forty 'rollers,
ranging in size from small merchants not much larger than
his own craft to tremendous three-decker 'rollers-of-the-line
from far-off Batrim, convoying even larger merchant vessels, high-pooped and richly decorated. Then, as they came
to within fifty miles of their destination, small pleasure
yachts appeared in increasing numbers. And by the time
they saw the white rocket-shaped towers that stretched from
horizon to horizon, Green was sweating at the manner in

which craft were shooting back and forth in front of him.

Miran said, "The entire nation is surrounded by these white towers and by many fortresses interspersed between them. Inside the great circle of towers the Estoryans have many rich farms on the plains. The city proper, however, is built on three roaming islands that were captured by their magic many centuries ago."

Green raised his eyebrows at this information. "Indeed? And where is the vessel that brought the two demons down from the skies?"

Miran looked blankly at the Earthman, though he knew well enough that he was keenly interested in the so-called demons.

"Oh, it is located close to the palace of the king himself, but not on the hills. It landed on the plain."

"Hmm. And the strangers will be burned during the Festival of the Eye of the Sun?"

"If they have lived, they will be."

Green didn't like to think about their dying. If they had, then his problem was solved. He stayed upon this planet and did the best he could here.

There was one thing he had to admit. That was that having Amra as his wife made such an event not so calamitous as it might have been. She'd keep him so interested that time would pass swiftly, even on this barbarous place.

In that case, he thought, why was he hesitating about taking her to Earth, if he got the chance? No matter where he was she'd see that life was a whirlpool of action. And she'd only begun to disclose the deeps within her. Give her an education, and what a creature might evolve!

What's the matter with you, Green? he said to himself. Don't you know your own mind? Are you so capable at handling physical events but a complete muckup when it comes to psychical? Why...?

"Look out!" cried Miran, and Green threw the helm hard

aport to avoid crashing into a small freighter. The captain, standing on the foredeck behind his own helmsman, leaned over the rail and shook his fist at Green and cursed. Green cursed back but after that he didn't allow himself to begin thinking about Amra until he had steered the 'roller into the 'break.

The rest of the day he was busy getting cleared with the port authorities. Fortunately he had a letter from the officer of the island-fortress. It explained why he happened to be in possession of a foreign craft and also recommended that Green be given a chance to sign up in the Estoryan 'roller-fleet if he wished. Even so, he had to tell his story so many times to an admiring and amazingly credulous audience that it was dusk before he could get free. Outside the customs building he found Grizquetr waiting for him.

"Where's your mother?" he asked.

"Oh, she knew you'd be tied up for a long time, so she went ahead and got a room in an inn. They're very hard to get during the Festival, almost impossible. But you know Mother," said Grizquetr, winking. "She gets what she goes after, every time."

"Yes, I'm afraid so. Well, where's this inn?"

"It's clear across town, but it's within sight of the wall that's built around the demons' skyship."

"Wonderful! Rooms must be twice as difficult to get there as on the edge of town. How did Amra do it?"

"She gave the innkeeper three times his asking price, which was high enough. And he found a pretext to quarrel with a man who had long ago reserved a room, threw him out and gave it to us!"

"Ah? And where did she get this money?"

"She sold a ruby to a jeweler who kept shop close to the 'break. He's sort of shady, I guess, and he didn't give Mother what the ruby was worth."

"Now, where would she get a ruby or any kind of jewel?"

Grizquetr grinned crookedly but delightedly. "Oh, I imagine that a certain fat one-eyed merchant-captain who shall remain nameless must have had one or two rubies within that bag he keeps inside his shirt."

"Yes, I can imagine. The question that alarms me is how did she get it off Miran? He'd sooner lose a quart of blood than one of his precious jewels. And he'd notice its loss quicker than he would the blood."

Grizquetr looked thoughtful. "I really don't know. Mother didn't say."

He brightened with a smile and said, "But I'd *like* to know how she did it! Maybe she'll teach me some day."

"She seems to have a lot to teach both of us," said Green.

He sighed. "Well, I'm eternally indebted to her. No getting out of it. Let's call a rickshaw and see what kind of a place she has selected."

Once both had settled in the high-backed chair of their vehicle, and the two men who pulled it had begun their slow trotting through the crowded streets, Green said, "Have you any idea where Miran is?"

"Some. He was detained by the port-officers, too, because he had to explain what had happened to his 'roller. Then he called a rickshaw and left in a big hurry. He had an officer with him. Not a naval officer. A soldier from the palace, one of the King's Own."

Green felt a sinking sensation. "Already? Tell me, does he know where we are staying?"

"Oh, no. When I saw him coming out of the customs-house, I hid behind a bale of cotton. Mother had told me to stay out of his sight. She explained how treacherous he is, and how he hates you because he thinks you brought all his bad luck upon him."

"That's only the half of it," Green replied. He was silent for a while, thinking, his gaze roving idly over the crowds. There were many foreigners in town, sailors from every nation that had a border on the Xurdimur, pilgrims who belonged to the far-flung cult of the Fish Goddess and had come here for the Festival. The majority, however, were Estoryans, a fairly tall people, brown or red-haired, green or blue-eyed, with big noses, thick lips and a slight epicanthic fold. They spoke a guttural polysyllabic semi-analytic language. They wore broad-rimmed hats shaped like open umbrellas, tight-necked shirts with long stingties and pants that were skintight from crotch to knee, then ballooned out into many ruffles. Little bells tinkled on their ankles, and the women carried canes. All had a fish, a star, or a rocket-shaped tower tattooed on their cheeks.

Along the narrow winding street were many little shops, flowering with a variety of articles. Green was intrigued by the magical charms being hawked everywhere. Many of these were little towers, replicas of the large ones that encircled the country. On Earth they could have passed for toy spaceships. He bought one. It was made of white-painted wood and was about seven inches long. The big flaring fins and landing struts were well reproduced, but there weren't any of the fine details that he could have found in such a toy on Earth. There were no holes in the stern or nose for the drive-exhaust or any indications of doors or detector apparatus.

He gave it to Grizquetr and leaned back to do some more thinking. The charm hadn't disappointed him, because he had not expected any more than what he'd seen. If, in the beginning, those models had been furnished with every little detail, the passage of many thousands of years would have seen them blunted and reduced to their present state of fuzzy symbolic images. Time ate down to the skeleton of things.

He wondered how the charm could have survived up to the present, because it surely must have been over twenty thousand years ago that the prototype, the real spaceship, disappeared and man sank back to savagery again. Then, why had this lasted here, whereas it had not done so on other planets, Earth included?

Abruptly, he noticed that his rickshaw had stopped.

"A procession of priests, going to the palace of the King, where they will spend all night preaching to the demon," said one of their rickshaw boys. He yawned and stretched. "I suppose that it will be a fine burning, since the priests have predicted that the sun will shine at high noon. They are safe doing that, as it has not failed to shine on Festival Day for a thousand years."

Green leaned forward, his hands gripping the sides of his chair, and said, "Demon? You meant demons, didn't you? Weren't there two of them?"

"Oh yes, there were. But one died two days ago. Hung himself, I heard, though I can't swear to it since the priests have released no details. The holy ones have been giving the demons a rough time."

"Demons?" said Grizquetr, snorting with disbelief and disgust. "Doesn't the very fact that one killed himself prove they're not fiends? Everyone knows that a demon can't kill himself."

"Quite true, my small friend," replied the taxi man. "The priests have admitted their error. They are truly sorry—so they say."

"Then aren't they letting the other man loose?"

"Oh no. Because *he* may still be a demon. Tomorrow, at high noon, the prisoner goes under the Sun's Eye and there meets the only death a demon may know. *By fire he was born, by fire he shall perish.* Chapter Twenty, Verse Sixty-Two. Or so I remember the High Grauchning saying in his sermon yesterday. Myself, I'm not much for reading. Too busy making a living, running my legs off, killing myself so my wife and kids may eat and have clothes on their backs."

Green scarcely heard the garrulous rickshaw man, so shocked was he at the news. Had he been too late? What if the man who'd died was the pilot and the other one unable to handle the ship?

The rest of the ride he was sunk in such deep gloom he hardly saw any of the many sights that Grizquetr kept pointing out. But he did rouse when the boy said, "Look, Father, there's the King's palace, on top of the hill! Beyond that is the ship of the demon. You can't see it from here, but you will tomorrow when you go to the burning."

"Don't be so heartless," said Green, but he looked carefully at the great marble structure that rambled all over the hill. Somewhere below that, probably filled with dirt, undoubtedly forgotten, was just such an entrance as he'd found on the island of the cannibals. He'd also discovered a similar one upon the fortress of Shimdoog, the night before when he'd gone exploring and Miran had followed him.

The palace, he thought, looked quite romantic and beautiful, enveloped in a dim red haze cast by the setting sun, which lay directly behind it. Probably it would look different in the harsh glare of day, when the dirt and garbage would be so apparent.

The area in which Amra had rented the room was one which had once belonged to the rich and the noble but had decayed when the aristocracy moved their homes elsewhere. The inn before which the rickshaw boys stopped was a three-story pile of granite blocks. It had an enormous porch and six huge pillars in the images of the Fish Goddess. Green could not help admiring the building even in its present state of decay, because he knew that it must have cost a fortune to build it. The granite would have had to be transported by 'roller across the Xurdimur, since there would be no stone in this neighborhood. He imagined that the landlord charged high rents and that Amra must have paid a pretty price indeed if she'd given him three times the usual amount. One thing you could say for her, when she traveled she did it in style.

The caryatids of the Fish Goddess also interested him, and at another time he'd have examined them closely by the light of the torches in the hands of the servants standing by them. The cult of the Goddess indicated that the original Estoryans must have migrated from the oceanside to the center of the vast and level plains. And here they must have built this imposing city, which was to become such a great focus of trade. Its central location made it a great clearing house for goods from every country bordering the Xurdimur.

He wondered whether it was pure accident that they had brought with them the charms in the shapes of spaceships? And if they'd also accidentally discovered that towers modeled after the charms would stop the roaming islands?

Whatever the answer, it lay buried in the prehistoric.

"Hurry up," said Grizquetr, pulling on Green's hand. "Mother has a surprise for you, but don't tell her I told you."

"That's nice," replied Green absently, his mind still upon the news of the Earthman's death. Hang it all, why must he always be kept in suspense, must always be improvising from moment to moment, always in the dark, never knowing what was coming next nor what he was going to have to do? Oh, for one day of peace and assurance!

"Father!"

"What, what?" said Green, startled out of his reverie and stopping halfway up the steps to the porch. Suddenly something black and small launched itself at him and landed on his shoulder.

"Lady Luck! Why are you shivering so?"

"Better run, Dad!" said Grizquetr. "There's Miran coming out of the door! And soldiers behind him!"

He ended with a wail, *"Motherr-r-r-r!"*

The sight of Amra, Inzax, and the children being marched out between musketmen was enough for Green. He turned away and spoke softly but savagely.

"Keep your backs to them! Don't look back! We're far enough away in the dark so they might not recognize us. Especially in this crowd!"

A minute later he and the boy and the cat were looking around the corner of a large building. They saw the soldiers commandeer a rickshaw and put the prisoners in it. Then four of them walked behind the vehicle as it was pulled away.

"They-they'll be put in the Tower of the Grass Cat," said the boy, shaking with fury. "Oh, that devil Miran! That fat old devil! He's the one who's accused Mother of witchcraft! I know! I know!"

"He didn't accuse her," said Green, "but me. She's guilty through association with me. Well at least we'll know where they are for a while."

"There go Miran and the soldiers back into the hotel."

"Waiting for us," said Green. "They'll have a long wait. Well, let's go. First things first. We'll buy a ticket, see the ship. I have to know where it's located, what type it is, et cetera. Luckily I've enough money on me to do that. But we'll be broke then. You have any?"

"Ten *axar*."

"That's not much, but it's enough to pay for a rickshaw ride to the windbreak."

At the box-office, Green bought two tickets, then walked up the steep flight of steps with Grizquetr. At the top he found himself in a large group standing on a platform beneath a wooden roof. This was for the curious who wanted to get a preview of the demons' vessel. Tomorrow the gates would be opened to admit a vast crowd, who would sit on the hard wooden seats of the amphitheatre that had been built fairly close to the ship.

The ship itself was an Earth naval vessel, a two-man scout. It pointed its needle nose upward, resting upon eight jet-struts, gleaming in the moonlight. Its naval insignia, a green globe crossed with rocket and olive branch, was a smudge in the shadows. Nevertheless he could make it out. He felt his breast swell and he choked with homesickness.

"Ah, so near, yet so far," he murmured. "Even if I get to you, then what? What if the poor devil of a survivor turns out to be a navigator? Still, he ought to know enough to get her off the ground and into space. And from there on, with interstellar drive, we ought to be able to get home, somehow."

He sounded plaintive, even to himself, for he knew how vast space was and how complicated astromathematics was. And of course there was no guarantee that the Earthman would even be a navigator. He might just be an officer or perhaps a civilian official who was being ferried in one of the swifter small ships.

Then there was the awful possibility that the vessel might have landed here because there was something wrong with it, and that it could not rise again even if it had a full crew. In fact, that was the most logical explanation.

He sighed and turned to the boy.

"This may be for nothing, but we can't just sit down and watch. Let's take off for the windbreak."

"What are we going to do there?" asked Grizquetr, as they walked down the steps.

"Well, we're not going back to the yacht," Green answered. "Soldiers'll be waiting there to arrest us. No, we'll go to the other side of the 'break. Stealing another 'roller isn't going to get us in any more trouble than we're already in."

The boy's eyes widened. "What're we doing that for?"

"We must return to the island-fortress of Shimdoog."

"What? Why, that's a hundred miles away!"

"Yes, I know. And we won't be able to make the speed going back that we did coming. We'll have to do quite a lot of tacking to sail against the wind, and that'll eat up our time. But there's nothing else to do."

"If you say so, father, I believe you. But what is there on Shimdoog?"

"Not on. *In.*"

Grizquetr was a bright lad. He was silent for a minute, so silent Green could imagine he heard the wheels turning within his head. Then he said, "There must be a cave on Shimdoog like the one on the cannibals' island. And you must have gone into it that night we stayed in the 'break. I remember waking up and hearing you and Mother say something about your being gone and about Miran following you."

Grizquetr paused, then said, "If there is a cave-entrance there, why haven't other people gone into it?"

"Because it has been declared taboo, off limits, by the priests of Estorya. It was done so long ago that I imagine that the priests themselves have forgotten why they forbade its access to men. But it's not hard to reconstruct the historical causes. Once, I suppose, the island was populated by cannibals. At the time the Estoryans captured the island they exterminated the aborigines. They found the cave mouth was a holy place for the savages. So, thinking that it held demons—and it does, in a way—they built a wall around it and set up a statue of the Fish Goddess, facing inward and holding in her hand a symbol to restrain the imprisoned fiends from breaking loose. That symbol, of course, is the same charm that is sold on the streets of Estorya, that circumscribes the country and the island of Shimdoog. It is the same as the spaceship that landed near the King's palace."

Green hailed a rickshaw and continued his account while they rode through the still-crowded streets. There was so much noise that he felt quite safe talking, provided he kept his voice soft.

By the time they had reached the northern end of the windbreak, Green had told the boy all he thought he should hear at that time. If, later on, his trip to Shimdoog proved successful he would enlighten him even more.

For the present he was concerned with the problem of getting transportation. Fortunately they found almost at once a nice little yacht with speedy lines and a tall mast. The craft must have belonged to a wealthy man, for a watchman sat close to it before a little fire just outside his shed. Green walked up to him, and when the fellow rose, his hand suspiciously resting upon his spear, Green struck him on the jaw, then followed with a hard right to the pit of his stomach. Grizquetr completed the job by hitting him over the head with a length of pipe he'd picked up off the ground.

Green emptied the handbag of the watchman and was pleased to see several coins of respectable denominations.

"Probably his life-savings," he said. "I hate to rob him, but we have to have money. Grizquetr, do you remember those slaves who were drinking and gambling outside the Striped Ape Inn? Run to them and offer them six *danken* if they'll tow us out of the 'break. Tell them we're paying them so much because it's so late at night, and also to keep their mouths shut."

Grinning, the boy ran off. Green hauled the limp body of the unconscious watchman behind the hut, bound and gagged him and threw a tarpaulin over him.

Grizquetr returned, leading six noisy and reeling men, sturdily built, with legs and backs big-muscled from hauling 'rollers.

At first Green thought he ought to try to make them keep quiet, then decided that it would look more natural if he let them talk as loudly as they wished. There was a festive air over the city tonight, and more than one yacht was going out for a moonlight cruise.

Once out on the plain, Green threw the promised money to the slaves and cried, "Have a good time!" To himself he muttered, "Because tomorrow may be your last day." Already, he had a presentiment of what might happen if he succeeded in tonight's work. There was no telling what forces he might be unloosing. As he'd said to the boy, there were demons imprisoned in the bowels of the island of Shimdoog.

26

JUST BEFORE DAWN the yacht coasted to a stop outside the high stone walls of the north side of the island of Shimdoog. Green had dropped the sail and, judging his speed exactly, had steered the craft until its side was almost scraping the wall. As soon as the roller stopped, Green put Lady Luck in a bag tied to his belt and cautioned her to keep quiet. Then he began climbing up the rungs nailed to the mast. The boy followed him, and both crawled out upon the spar. Green tied one end of a long rope around the end of the spar. Then he let himself down on it to the ground on the other side of the wall.

After the boy had also descended they paused for a moment, crouched, ready to run at the first sign they'd been seen. But there was no outcry.

The big moon, though dropping to the horizon, was bright

enough for them to make good progress. Green led the way up a series of hills, heading in a circuitous fashion toward the highest. Twice he had to stop and warn Grizquetr about the towers ahead, where sentries were stationed. Lady Luck seemed to know she should be silent. Her eyes glowed and her teeth flashed, but she was only making a soundless snarl.

They saw the fires of the guards and heard their muttered voices, but none saw them. It was doubtful that the sentinels ever did look out, for they did not think that any man in his right senses would be roaming about in the darkness, where it was well-known that ghosts and demons waited for foolish mortals.

Just before they began climbing the slope of the peak that was their goal, Green whispered. "This island is built much like the first one we encountered. I think that all of these islands are more or less similar, all being composed of a base of a mile and a half square of eternum metal or something like eternum. And all covered with rock and dirt and trees and vegetation and stocked with birds and beasts. I suppose that the original builders landscaped these craft for aesthetic reasons. After all, a sheet of metal with a few metal chambers on it doesn't look very pretty and would make a blinding glare in the sunshine."

"Uh," replied the boy, who didn't understand.

"Do you know, it's strange that I was right the first time when I sarcastically referred to the roaming islands as glorified lawn-mowers?"

"What?"

"Yes, in the beginning there must have been many more than there are now, enough to keep the vast plains looking neat and well-kept, the grass clipped, the forests prevented from encroaching well-defined limits, and so on. But when there were no longer any maintenance men to keep them going, they stopped, one by one, until at this present time there are perhaps a few hundred. Though, I don't know, there may be more. Anyway, whenever one did run down or break down for some reason or other it was soon erased by a still-functioning island."

"Erased?"

"Yes, for it's quite obvious to me that the islands not only cut grass, they kept the plains free of obstructions that weren't supposed to be there. And a dead island would constitute just such a hazard."

Grizquetr spoke in a thin voice, "Perhaps, Father, I may yet understand you. I must be stupid."

"Far from it. You'll learn in time. Anyway, I should have known what they really were when I heard the tales of the sailors. Remember that one about the big hole made by the meteorite? And how something mysterious filled it in and covered it with turf? And then there was the way that wrecked 'rollers would vanish down to the last nut and bolt and the skeletons of the dead aboard. And there was the legend of Samdroo the Tailor Turned Sailor and what he found in the metal chambers inside an island. The great white eye through which he saw what was outside the island. And the other paraphernalia. They weren't the property of a wicked magician, as the tale would have it. Any Earthman would recognize TV and radar and dials and controls."

"Tell me more."

"I will when we get over this wall."

Green had stopped before a barrier of stone, reaching at least forty feet high. A grim crown, it completely encircled the top of the hill. "Once it must have been difficult to scale, but mortar has crumbled here and there, and vines grow all the way up. Follow me. I remember exactly the path I took."

He jumped up on a little ledge, seized a thick vine and hauled himself up to another minor projection. Unhesitatingly, the boy swarmed up after him.

Panting, they reached the top, where they rested a moment and wiped the blood from their lacerated fingertips.

The cat was the only one that seemed unperturbed. Silently, Green pointed out the twenty foot high statue of the Fish Goddess below, her back turned to them as she gestured at the cave mouth with the rocket-shaped charm.

For the first time Grizquetr seemed scared. Like all his fellows, he had an unhealthy awe for the supernatural. This place, so walled off, so utterly ancient-looking, so invested with all the attributes of taboo, so invocative of the horrible tales of demons and angry gods, depressed him. Only his father's seeming indifference to any fiends they might encounter kept him from turning tail and backing down the wall.

"One thing I'll bet, and that is that Miran didn't follow me this far but stayed down on the ground. With that belly of his he'd never have made it; he'd have tumbled off like a big fat bug and been squashed like one, too. Wouldn't that have been awful! However, he didn't have to go all the way with me. The very fact that I would dare to enter a taboo area is enough to condemn me. I should have slit his throat when Amra told me he'd been shadowing me. But I couldn't do it without absolutely convincing evidence, and even if I'd had that I suppose I'm too civilized to kill him in cold blood."

"You should have told me how you felt," said Grizquetr. "I would have slipped a dagger through the tallow over his ribs."

"No doubt, and so would your mother. Well, down we go."

And he set the example by throwing his leg over the edge of the wall and letting himself down, somewhat gingerly. The descent was even worse than the ascent, but he didn't bother telling the boy that. By the time he found out he'd be at the bottom.

Even so, when he reached ground, he thought that the lad couldn't be one whit more shaky than he. Forty feet was a long, long way when you were up on top looking down, especially in the moonlight.

"This is the second time I've done it, but I don't think I'd have guts enough for a third time," said Green.

"But we have to climb back out, don't we?"

"Oh, we'll have to go over it, but I hope it won't be so high by then," said Green, looking mysterious.

"What do you mean?"

"Well I hope those stones will all be tumbled to the ground. In fact, it's a necessity, if we're to do what I expect to do."

He took the bewildered boy by the hand and led him past the cold and silent statue and into the cave's entrance. "We could use a light," he said, "but a torch would have been too awkward to carry up that wall, and we can grope our way to the rooms that are lighted."

Wonder why the passageway wasn't lighted, too? he thought. Or had this cave been added by the savages who used to live on the island, so that the *sanctum sanctorum* would have to be approached through darkness? Perhaps it was, the primitives having constructed such a chamber so that the initiate into the religion could go through darkness both literal and symbolical and come into a light that also embraced both worlds? He didn't and couldn't know; he could only guess.

But I can take advantage of what I do have on hand, he said to himself, gritting his teeth with determination.

The dust beneath his feet gave way to clean metal. They rounded a corner and found themselves in a chamber much like the one upon their first island, except that this had furniture. A skeleton lay in the middle of the floor, face down. The back of the skull exhibited a great hole.

"He may have been here for a thousand years or more," said Green. "I'd like to know his story. But I never will."

"Do you think the Goddess killed him?"

"No, nor the demons either. It was the hand of man struck him down, my boy. If it's violent death you're trying to explain, don't drag in the supernatural. There's enough murder in the hearts of humankind to take care of every case."

In the third room Green said, "There's no wall of dust to stop us. The ionic charges haven't stopped working. Notice how clean everything is. Ah, here we are! Before the door!"

Grizquetr looked puzzled. "Door? I see only a blank wall."

"That's all I saw too," said Green, "and that is all I would ever have seen if it hadn't been for the tale of Samdroo."

"Let me tell you how you got in!" chattered the boy excitedly. "I know what you were thinking of, what you did. You stood before the wall and you made a sign like this on it!"—He traced a rough outline of a rocket against the cool white metal—"and the wall suddenly slid to one side, and you had an entrance. See!"

A whole section had moved noiselessly into the wall, leaving a round doorway.

"Yes, I remembered the story of Samdroo and, though it was ridiculous to think that it would work, I did what the Sailor did. Remember that the cannibals were after him, and he ran into the cave and came to just such a blank wall. And he, wishing to protect himself against the evil spirits that he was sure lived in the cave, traced the sign that is supposed to prevent them from touching a man. And the door slid open and he plunged on into the chambers of the wicked magician, the savages howling frustratedly after him."

"And," continued Green, "I did just what he did, and the sign proved to be an *Open, O Sesame* for me."

"A what?"

"Never mind. The point is that the ancient maintenance men must have used just such a gesture to open the door, or else used it in conjunction with other means. And if they did, then they must also have been repair technicians for the ships that landed here. Perhaps the sign of the rocket was a secret symbol for their guild. I don't know, but it sounds reasonable."

Ignoring the boy's flood of questions, he walked into a great room. It was more bare than he'd expected when he had found it the first time; it contained four machines or their fuel supplies, all concealed in four large square metal containers. In the center of the room was a chair and an instrument panel. The panel contained six TV windows, several oscilloscopes, and dials whose purpose he didn't know. But the controls attached to the arms of the chair seemed simple enough.

"The only trouble," he said, "is that I don't know where the activating switch is. I tried to find it the other night and couldn't. Yet, it must be so obvious that I'll feel like a fool when I do locate it."

Vainly he pulled at the little levers set in the arms.

"My failure to activate this was the main reason I returned to the yacht and sailed on to Estorya. Of course, I had to go and find out just what the situation was and get a good idea of my plan of campaign. Perhaps if I'd stayed here and taken a chance on going into the city blind, we'd have been better off. At least, your mother wouldn't now be in prison, and we wouldn't have the additional worry of rescuing her."

He rose from the chair and began pacing back and forth.

"How ironic if I'd come this far and could get no farther! But then, what else could I expect? It's up to me to solve this, and I'm not infallible, omniscient. It should be functioning as of now. I know that the ring of rocket-shapes has got it paralyzed so it can't act. Nevertheless, unless it's blown a fuse, gone neurotic from frustration, or just worn out, there should be some indication that it is still in operation."

"What do you mean?" said Grizquetr. "How can the island be paralyzed?"

Green stopped pacing to gesture at the radarscopes. "See those? Well, there should be some funny lines squiggling across it, or little dots moving, or arcs sweeping across it. They would be indicating the shapes of things in the immediate neighborhood outside the island, and the lay of the land. Thus, I imagine that in the ancient days, when it spotted a rocket shape, which would then have been a genuine spaceship and not a mockup, it would have detoured around it. The whole island was, in one of its functions, a field attendant, a scavenger. It removed anything from the plain that wasn't supposed to be there. There's why they now attack 'rollers and crush them and disintegrate the parts that fall beneath their bases. That also explains why the island is trapped by a ring of rocket-shaped towers. The radar detects a complete circle and, being unable to molest any object shaped like a rocket, it squats in one place until it runs down or the rocket shapes are removed.

"Of course, it worked automatically. But there were controls for a man to operate it when there was a special job to do or if he had to take it to another place it ordinarily wouldn't go when on automatic. These controls must be the ones.

"The question is, does the island switch itself off and on at certain intervals, scanning the area around it to see if the inhibiting objects have gone? If so, there's no telling how long we may have to wait before its next sweep. And we just can't afford to wait!"

He was in agony. As long as he could keep his body and brain in action, he felt he was progressing. But as soon as he had to wait upon some inanimate object that he couldn't attack, or came across a seemingly unsolvable problem, he was lost. He just didn't have the patience.

Lady Luck whined. She was tired of being imprisoned

in the bag at Green's waist and felt that she had been a good girl long enough.

Absently, he lifted her out and put her on the table. She stretched, yawned, licked her lips, and then padded across the table. Her tail switched back and forth, and its tip brushed the surface of the centrally located TV screen.

Immediately, a metal ball on the panel glowed red and a sharp whistle sounded. Two seconds later, light sprang into being in all of the viewers.

27

"OH, YOU BEAUTY, YOU DOLL, you lovely Lady Luck! Whatever would I do without you!" shouted Green. He started forward to caress the cat, but, alarmed, she jumped from the table and sped across the room.

"Come back, come back!" he called. "I wouldn't hurt a single one of your lovely black hairs! I'll feed you on beer and fish the rest of your life, and you'll never have to put in a day's work!"

"What's the matter?" said Grizquetr.

Green hugged him, then sat down in the chair.

"Nothing, except that that wonderful cat showed me how to activate the equipment. You do so by brushing your hand across this screen. See, I'll bet you do the same when you want to deactivate it!"

He touched the screen. The whistle sounded again, the

metal ball ceased glowing and the screens went dead. Once again he touched it, and life came back.

"Nothing to it. But chances are I'd never have found out how simple it was."

He began sobering up. "Down to work. Let's see..."

The six TV windows showed them the north, east, south, west, above and below. As the island was resting upon solid dirt there was, of course, nothing to see beneath.

"We'll remedy that. But first I think we'd better see if these screens give expanding and contracting views."

He fiddled around with the levers. When he depressed the second one, the room jumped. Hastily replacing it in neutral, Green said, "Well, we know what that one does. I'll bet the people outside think they had a slight earthquake. They've seen nothing yet. Hmmm. Here, I think, is the one I want."

He twisted a knob on the right-hand arm. All the TV's began narrowing their field of vision. Reversing the knob, however, made them spread out their view, though the objects in them, of course, became smaller.

It took him five minutes more of cautious testing before he felt justified in beginning operations. Then he raised the island off the ground about twenty feet and rocked it back and forth. Lady Luck leaped for his lap and cowered down in it. Grizquetr, bracing himself against the table, turned pale.

"Relax, kid," called Green. "As long as you're going along on the ride you might as well enjoy it."

Grizquetr grinned feebly, but when his father told him to stand behind him so he, too, could learn how to operate, he gained color and confidence.

"When we get to Estorya I may have to leave this chamber, and I'll need somebody who can see me through the TVs and answer my signals. You're the candidate. You may be only a kid, but anybody who can calmly talk of slipping a knife through a man's ribs has what it takes."

"Thank you," breathed Grizquetr in all sincerity.

"Here's what I'll do," said Green. "I'll roll this island back and forth until the soldiers are thoroughly panicky and seasick. And the walls around the cave are tumbled down. Then we'll lower to earth again and give the rats a chance to desert the ship. But we're no sinking ship, not us. After everybody that's able has fled to the plains, we'll take off at top speed for Estorya."

Fascinated, the boy watched the screens and saw the soldiers run off into the early morning light, yelling, their eyes and mouths bulging with horror. Some, wounded, crawled off.

"I feel sorry for them," said Green, "but somebody's got to get hurt before this is over and I'd rather it wasn't us."

He pointed to the 'scopes, which still indicated the ring of towers.

"As long as this island was on automatic it couldn't pass those inhibitories. But I've bypassed that with this switch. Now, we go ahead, and not over the towers, as we could easily do, but through them. I think we've got the weight behind us."

There was a slight shock, the rooms trembled, then the towers before them were gone and they were speeding across the plain. Minute by minute Green increased their rate, until he thought they must be making about a hundred and twenty-five miles an hour.

"Those dials are probably telling me my speed," he said to Grizquetr. "But I can't read their alphabet or numerical system. It doesn't matter."

He laughed as he watched 'rollers wheel hard aport or hard to starboard in a frenzy to get out of their way. The rails and ratlines were lined with white faces, like rags of terror fluttering in the breeze of the island's passage.

"If there were time to send a message, I imagine we'd

encounter the whole Estoryan fleet," said Green. "What a battle that would be! Rather, what a massacre, for this craft is built for eating up whole navies."

"Father," said Grizquetr, "we could be king over the whole world, we could rule the Xurdimur and take tribute off every 'roller that sailed!"

"Yes, I suppose we could, you little barbarian, you," replied Green. "But we won't. We're using this for just one purpose, rescuing the Earthman and your mother and sisters. After that . . ."

"Yes?"

"I don't know."

He fell into a reverie as the plain beneath raced past, the white sails of the 'rollers blooming from small patches to great flags, then dwindling as swiftly.

Finally, rousing from his thoughts, he began to explain a little to the boy.

"You see, many thousands of years ago there was a great civilization that had many machines that would seem to you even more magical than this one. They traveled to the stars and there found worlds much like this one, and they put colonies upon them. They had swift ships that could jump across the vast abyss between these worlds and so keep in fairly close touch.

"But something happened, some catastrophe. I can't imagine what it could be, but it must have happened. While it would be interesting to know the cause, all we can know is the effect. Travel ceased, and as time went by the colonies, which were probably rather small to begin with, lost their civilization. The colonies must have been rather dependent upon supplies shipped to them, and they must have had a limited number of highly trained scientists and specialists among them. Anyway, whatever the reason, they relapsed into savagery. And it was not until ages had passed that some of these colonies, utterly without memory of their glorious heritage, except perhaps disguised in myth and legend, attained a high technology again. Others stayed in savagery; some, like your world, Grizquetr, are in the transition stage. Your culture is roughly analogous to the ones that existed on Earth between 100 A.D. and 1000 A.D. Those dates mean nothing to you, I know, but let me assure you that we present-day Terrestrials regard those times as being, well, rather hazardous and, uh, unreasonable in their conduct."

"I only half-understand you," replied the boy. "But didn't you say that nothing of the wisdom of the ancients survived on your planet? Well, why had it done so on ours? These islands must be the work of the old ones."

"Correct! And that's not all. So is the Xurdimur itself."

"What?"

"Yes, it's obvious to me that this planet must once have been a tremendous clearinghouse and landing field for spacecraft. These plains couldn't be natural; they must have been leveled out by machinery. A laboratory-born grass was planted that had all the characteristics needed to hold the soil together and keep erosion away. Plus the fact that the islands themselves were, you might say, caretakers, and kept the whole field spruced up.

"Gods! I can imagine what a traffic this planet must have had to build such a landing-field! Ten thousand miles across! The mind boggles before the thought. They must have done things on a big scale then. Which makes it all the more difficult to figure out how they could have come to ruin. Will we ever know what force wrecked them?"

Grizquetr, of course, had even less of an answer than Green. Both were silent for a while; then they cried out simultaneously when the pointed tips of the white towers surrounding Estorya glittered upon the horizon. One of the screens began flashing a series of cone shapes that indicated the towers.

"If the island were still on automatic it would be forced to go around the entire nation," said Green. "But I'm running it now, and we're paying no attention to those towers."

"Knock 'em down!"

"That's just what I intend to do. But not right now. Let's see. Wonder how high we can go. Only one way to find out. Upsydaisy!"

He pulled back the lever and the island began rising, though still maintaining its horizontal attitude.

"The ancients, like us moderns, knew how to build antigravity machines. And they also must have kept building their spaceships in the conventional rocket-form long after there was any need for it. Perhaps, though, they did so in order for the islands to have a more definite radar image. Maybe. No one really knows."

He spoke to himself, meanwhile glancing at the screen which showed him the plains and the city of Estorya beneath, ever-dwindling as their height increased.

"Do me a favor, Grizquetr. Run out to the cave's mouth and tell me if those walls have fallen over. And on your way back, close the door to this room. It's going to get colder very quickly, and the air will be thin. But I imagine that this room is equipped with automatic heat and oxygen. If it isn't I want to find out now."

The boy began running back. "The walls are all shaken down, all right!" he said breathlessly. "And the Fish Goddess fell over, and her head almost blocks up the cave's mouth. I wriggled through without any trouble. I think you can squeeze through."

Green felt a little sick. That possibility had not occurred to him. It would have been ironic if the statue had completely blocked the entrance and he'd had to stay inside until he starved to death. The Estoryans, of course, would have considered his death a case of poetical justice. . . . No, he wouldn't have died, either! He'd just have gone back to the controls and rolled the island over on one side until the statue's head came loose. But what if the big stone blocks from the tumbled wall had fallen down behind the statue so that they wedged her too tightly to be released? He sweated at the thought and glanced fondly at the black cat. He wasn't superstitious, not at all, but it seemed to him that his luck had been better since she'd adopted him. Of course, that wasn't the scientific attitude to take; nevertheless he felt comforted just knowing she was around.

By now, the whole nation of Estorya could be encompassed in one glance. And the sky was getting darker.

"We're high enough." He stopped the island. "If anybody didn't get off, he must be dead by now, the air's so thin. And I was right. We do have automatic heat and air-providers. Very comfortable in here. I only wish we had something to eat."

"Why not lower us to the height where I can go out and find food in the garrison's kitchens?" said Grizquetr. "Nobody'll be alive to stop me."

Green thought that was an excellent suggestion. He was very hungry, for he always had to eat for two, himself and the Vigilante. If the symbiote within his body provided him with more than normal strength and powers, it also demanded fuel on which to operate. And, deprived of food, it would survive by living upon Green's tissue. A Vigilante wasn't all advantage; it had its dangers.

He lowered the island to about two thousand feet, set the controls on neutral, then decided that it would be safe to go out with the boy. Just as he got to the doorway, however, he began feeling uneasy and wondering what he would do if, somehow, the door closed and he couldn't get it open again. That would be a fine situation, to be stuck two thousand feet in the air, and no parachute!

Perhaps he was silly, absurdly apprehensive, but he wasn't going to take any more chances. Grinning sheepishly, he told the boy to go on by himself. He'd decided to study the controls more closely and think out his strategy in finer detail.

When Grizquetr returned with a basket loaded with food and wine, Green swore at himself for his moment's weakness, then forgot it. After all, discretion was the better part and all that, and he was only playing it smart.

Greedily, he devoured the food and drank half a bottle of wine, knowing the Vigilante would use alcohol before food and that little of it would remain in his bloodstream before being consumed. Between bites, he told Grizquetr what he planned.

"We'll descend as soon as we're finished eating. I'll write a note, and you'll drop it over the side upon the steps of the palace. The note will inform the King he'd better release his prisoners, unharmed, just outside the windbreak. There we may easily pick them up and then take off like the proverbial big bird. If he refuses we will proceed to lower the island upon the Temple of the Fish Goddess, crushing it and her jewel-encrusted golden idol. And if he still isn't convinced we'll then smash the palace, not to mention toppling over the entire ring of towers around the country. Of course, before we drop the note we'll knock over a few anyway just to show him we're not bluffing."

Grizquetr's eyes shone. "Can the island crush a big building?"

"Yes, though I think that there's a possibility we could as easily disintegrate it. I've wondered how the island cut the grass, and can only conclude that it must use a device similar to one we have on Earth. It cuts through objects by breaking up their atomic structure with a beam that is only a molecule-thick. When on grass-cutting duty, the island must emit such a beam, and only beneath its base. Of course, it must have other machines, too, for cleaning up wreckage and debris and other stuff that its memory banks tell it has no business being on the field. But I don't know to operate these."

Grizquetr looked reproachfully at Green.

"Well, I don't know everything. I'm not a superman, am I?"

The boy did not reply, but his expression conveyed the idea that he thought his foster-father was just that. Green shrugged his shoulders and sent the boy out to get paper, pen and ink from the garrison. By the time the boy returned, Green had lowered the island to about fifty feet above the palace. He hastily wrote a note, put it in the basket, which had a cover that could be snapped shut, and told Grizquetr to throw it over the side, aiming at the steps.

"I know you're going to be worn out with all this running back and forth," he said, "but you can do it. You're big and strong."

"Sure I am," said the boy. Chest expanded, he dashed from the room, almost tripped going through the door, recovered, and disappeared. Grinning, Green began to watch the crowds that had gathered below. Presently he saw the basket hurtle toward a group of priests upon the great stairway. His grin broadened when the group disintegrated in panic and several of them lost their footing and rolled down the steps.

He waited until one of them got enough courage to return and open the basket. Then he lowered the island another twenty feet. At the same time, he saw a cannon being hauled into the square before the palace and its nose being raised so that it could fire upon him.

"Have to give the beggars credit for guts," he murmured. "Or for sheer folly, I don't know which. Well, fire away, friends."

They didn't, because a priest came running to stop them.

Evidently, his note, though written in Huinggro, had been translated swiftly enough, and the Estoryans were taking no hasty action.

"While we're waiting for them to make up their minds we'll give them a taste of the feast they can expect if they aren't reasonable," Green said.

He then proceeded to push over about twenty towers just outside the windbreak. It was great fun, and he'd have liked to knock down a hundred or so more, but he was too anxious to find out about Amra and the Earthman. He returned to his former vigil above the palace steps.

Impatiently, he waited for ten minutes that seemed like ten hours. Finally, when he could bear it no longer, he growled, "I'm going to squat on the roof of the Temple and make them hurry up. Do they think this is a diplomatic conference or something, that they can dillydally about like this?"

"No, father," said Grizquetr. "There they come! Mother and Paxi and Soon and Inzax! And a strange man! He must be the demon!"

"Demon, your horned hoof!" snorted Green. "That man's as human as I am. And the poor fellow must have gone through hell. Even from this height I can see he looks bad. Look how he has to be supported between two soldiers."

Amra and the others, he was happy to note, seemed to be unharmed.

Nevertheless he was anxious about them during their ride through the city's streets and out to the windbreak. The Estoryans might have plans for a sudden attack, though he didn't see how they could expect to surprise him, since from his vantage point, he would notice any concentration of troops immediately. Or, a fanatical priest might take it into his head to kill them.

Neither of these possibilities happened. The prisoners were released outside the fallen towers, and the soldiers retreated into the city. Grizquetr left the control room to guide them onto the island. In fifteen minutes he ran back.

"Here they are, Father! Saved! Now, get off the ground before the Estoryans change their minds."

"We're going back," replied Green, looking in vain for the others and then deciding that the boy had outstripped them in his haste to report. He shoved the lever forward and the ship—he was beginning to think of the island as a ship—soared toward the cone of the spacecraft, which he could see glittering in the sun inside its wall near the palace. When Amra and the girls ran into the chamber and wished to throw their arms around him, he told them he'd be very glad to give each a big warm kiss later on. Right now he had work to do.

Amra's smile was replaced by a frown.

"Do you mean you're still thinking of leaving on the demon's ship?" she said harshly.

"That depends on certain factors about which I don't have enough information as yet to act on," he replied, somewhat stiffly.

The Earthman limped in. He was a tall, broad-shouldered but emaciated man. His bushy beard made his long, lean, big-eared, hawk-nosed face resemble Lincoln's.

"Captain Walzer of the Terrestrial Interstellar Fleet, Intelligence," he said, weakly.

"Alan Green, marine food specialist. I've a long story to tell and no time to tell it. I would like to know if you can pilot that spacer and if it's in operating condition. Otherwise we might as well forget it and go elsewhere."

"Yes, I'm the pilot. Hassan was the navigator and communications officer. Poor devil, he died in agony! Those beasts...!"

"I know how you feel, but we've no time to go into that. Is the ship ready to take off?"

Walzer sat down and leaned his head wearily to one side.

Grizquetr offered him wine, and he took two long swallows and smacked his lips before replying.

"Ah, that's the first drink I've had for two years! Yes, the bird's ready to take off on a moment's notice. We'd been on a mission whose purpose I can't tell you. Security, you know. We were returning when we encountered this system. Since it's part of our duty to report any T-type planet if we've time, we decided to stop off and stretch our legs. We'd been in space so long we were beginning to suffer from claustrophobia and were ready to fly at each other's throats. You know how it is if you've made any very long voyages. And those scouts have especially cramped quarters. They're not made for long trips, but the nature of our mission required the use of one ... well, we won't go into that.

"Anyway, we were wild to breathe fresh air again, to see a horizon, to feel grass beneath our bare feet, to go swimming, to eat freshly killed meat and freshly picked fruit. We rationalized ourselves into the idea that it was our duty to land. We decided on this city because it was so conspicuous, stuck out here in the middle of this incredible plain. And, of course, when we got close enough to see that it seemed to be surrounded by a ring of spaceships we had to enter the city itself and inquire about this phenomenon. We were greeted friendlily enough, lulled into being off guard, then attacked. The rest of the story you know."

Green nodded and said, "Here we are. Just above the ship."

He rose from the chair and faced the group. "But before we take any further steps I think we ought to thrash out something right now that has been bothering Amra and me. Tell me, Walzer, is there enough room for Amra, Paxi, Soon, Grizquetr and myself? And perhaps for Inzax, if she wished to come along?"

Walzer's eyes widened. "No, man, absolutely not! There's

barely space for you, let alone anybody else."

Green held out his hands to Amra. "You see? I was afraid of this all the time. I'll have to go without you."

He paused, swallowed, then said, "But I'll return! I swear I will! I'll get the Interstellar Archaeology Bureau interested in this planet. When I tell them of the Xurdimur, of the rocket-shaped towers, of the islands with their anti-gravity machines, they'll not hesitate a moment in organizing an expedition. The chance of solving the mystery of how man spread all over the Galaxy in prehistoric times will be too strong for them.

"And I'll come back with them. And I'll make this planet my life work. I've a Ph.D. in ichthyology, and I can get accredited as a scientific member of the expedition. There's no doubt about it!"

Amra fell into his arms, weeping, crying that she had known all the time that he couldn't leave her. Then in the next breath she was swearing that he was just promising to return so he would avoid a scene.

"I know men well, Alan Green, and I know you, especially. You won't come back!"

"Yes, I will, I swear it. If you know men so well, you ought to know that no man who is worthy of being called a man could even think of leaving a woman like you."

She smiled through her tears and said, "That's what I wanted to hear you say. But, oh, Alan, it'll be so long. Won't it take at least two years?"

"Yes, at least. But it can't be helped. I'll worry about you while I'm gone. Or I would if I didn't know how capable you were."

"I can learn how to run this island," she said half-sobbing, half-smiling. "By the time you get back I'll probably be Queen of the Xurdimur. I could contact the Vings, and together we could have the whole plain and every city along its border under our thumbs. And . . ."

He laughed and said, "That was what I was afraid of."

Turning to Walzer, he said, "Look, you're too weak to consider another long trip immediately. Why don't you just follow this island in your ship until we get to a safe distance from here, say about a thousand miles due north? We'll live on the island until you get your strength back and get over your claustrophobia. I imagine it wasn't helped any by being cooped up in that dungeon. When you're ready we'll take off. In the meantime I can be showing Amra and Grizquetr just what can be done with the island. She can be living on it while I'm gone. We'll trap wild life to replace the animals that were strangled when I went up too high for them to breathe. She can shuttle back and forth over the Xurdimur, or over the whole planet if she wishes. And she will, I hope, stay out of mischief until I get back."

"That's fine," said Walzer. "I'll get in the ship and follow you."

Three weeks later, the two Earthmen boarded the scout and closed the port behind them, the port that would not open again until they were on Earth, some four months subjective time away. They sat down in the control cabin, and Walzer began pushing buttons and throwing switches.

Green wiped the sweat from his brow, the tears from his eyes, and said, "Whew!"

"A fine woman," said Walzer sympathetically. "A rare beauty. She has a tremendous impact upon one."

"Something like crashing into a planet head-on," said Green. "She has the faculty of wringing out every last bit of energy left in the particular emotion she happens to be feeling at the moment. A great actress who believes in her roles."

"Her children are fine children, too," Walzer added, slowly and as if he were about to say something that might hurt Green's feelings but was anxious not to do so. "You will be glad to see them again, of course."

"Of course. After all, Paxi's my daughter, I love the others as if they were also mine."

"Ah," breathed Walzer. "Then you *are* going back to her?"

Green didn't express surprise or anger, because he had guessed from Walzer's actions just what he was thinking.

"You can't imagine my wanting to live on that barbaric planet with that woman, can you?" he said, evenly. "That after all, there are serious gaps in our ways of thinking, in our behavior, in our education. Isn't that what you meant by your statement?"

Walzer glanced out of the corners of his eyes at Green, then replied warily, "Well, yes. But you know what you want far better than I do." He paused, then added, "I must say I admire your courage."

Green shrugged.

"After all I've been through I'm not afraid to take one more chance."